ENTWINED IN YOU, BOOK TWO

ASHLEE ROSE

SOMETHING TO LOSE
Copyright © 2018 Ashlee Rose
First Edition

To everyone who believed in me and told me to
not give up when it got tough,
This is for you X

CHAPTER ONE

When would this empty feeling leave? My heart, torn into a thousand pieces. I had been replaying what happened over and over again. I hadn't heard much from Carter, but to be honest, he had probably given up. The text messages and phone calls he made were just ignored by me. I had nothing to say to him.

"Sweetie, here. Take this." My mum smiled at me, handing me a hot cup of tea. I smiled weakly back at her. It had been two weeks but I just couldn't see myself getting over this. I didn't feel like this when Jake cheated on me, and we were together for so long. I had only been with Carter for a month or so, yet this time seemed to hurt even more.

My mum walked back over to me. She sat next to me and pulled me into her embrace. "I promise you, darling, it will all be okay." She kissed me on the forehead.

I heard footsteps and my dad appeared. "Love you, baby face," he said with a smile.

He flicked on the TV; *The Proposal* was on. I snuggled into my mum and pulled my duvet up; Ryan Reynolds always makes everything better.

I woke the next morning and stretched out. I reached over for my phone: another text from Ethan, two from Laura, a couple from Rachel, and one from Brooke. Tilly walked up the bed; she must have known I needed a cuddle. She padded her paws into my chest and snuggled under my chin, purring. I smiled. Mum never allowed me to have pets growing up, so this was big for her. I knew she was struggling having Tilly there, but Mum knew she would cheer me up.

I finally pulled myself out of bed and into our bathroom. My mum had run a bath for me. I dropped my pyjamas to the floor and slowly slid into the bath. I let out a big sigh as my skin soaked in the hot water. *You need to sort yourself out, Freya. Get over it.* I sighed at my subconscious. The bitch. I slid under the water and let the bath water take over. I felt so relaxed. It had been two weeks since everything happened. I wanted to get my life back. I didn't want to be moping around like a stroppy teenager, but I honestly thought this was it for me and Carter. I thought he was my prince. Obviously not. I rose from the water and wrung out my hair. I stepped out of the bath, wrapped my towel around me, and walked over to the vanity unit. I put my hands either side of the sink and let out a deep breath. I looked up at my reflection. "Freya, where the hell are you?" I mumbled. I shook my head. I needed to get dressed and go out. Laura and Tyler were staying at her mum and dad's. They got back from their honeymoon yesterday so that would help take my mind off everything.

I walked back into my old bedroom and went through my wardrobe. I pulled out my good old River Island jeans, Converse, and an oversized t-shirt which I tucked into the front of my jeans. I pulled my hair into a messy bun and pulled a few strands out. I put some lip balm on and applied a thin layer of mascara. It was the 1st September. It was still warm, but there was a chilly wind in the air. I picked up my phone, kissed Tilly, and pulled my door behind me. I typed a quick message to Laura saying I was on my way then locked my phone screen and put my phone in my tatty bag. I walked down the stairs and left my bag by the front door. I walked through the living room, looking for my parents.

They were sitting around the dining room table with their cups of tea, Dad reading the paper and listening to his favourite radio station, Mum playing her word game on her phone. I cleared my throat. "Morning," I said quietly.

They both looked at each other, then at me, and smiled. "Hey, baby face." My dad beamed. My parents looked at each other and gave a sympathetic smile.

"It's nice to see you dressed, darling," Mum said.

I smiled at her. "It feels good to be dressed." I looked down at my feet and put my hand in my back pocket. "Erm, so I'm going to pop to Lucinda and Gary's. Laura and Tyler got back from their honeymoon yesterday so I thought it would do me good to go up and see them. Be nice to talk about something other than me." I laughed to myself.

My mum stood from the table and walked over to me. "Don't be silly. It's good to talk." She kissed me on the cheek then sat back down at the table and took my dad's hand, smiling.

I picked my bag up and shouted out to my parents as I shut the door. I stood on the doorstep and inhaled deeply, standing still for about five minutes, just watching the world go by. I took a slow walk to Laura's parents'. I looked around our little village, reminiscing about my childhood. Before I knew it, I was standing outside

Lucinda and Gary's. I walked slowly up their pathway. Last time I was there, it was Laura's wedding morning. I knocked on the door then knotted my fingers as I waited anxiously. She didn't text me back, so I just assumed she would be there.

Just as I was about to walk away, Lucinda opened the door. "Hey, Freya." She smiled sympathetically at me and pulled me in for a hug. She pulled away and kissed me on the cheek. "How are you feeling?"

I smiled at her. "Not too bad. I've been better, you know?" I shrugged.

She just nodded. She looked over her shoulder when she heard Gary approaching. "Hey, Freya. So nice to see you." He walked over to me and kissed me on the cheek.

"Tyler has had to go to work, some emergency in the market. Laura is upstairs." He stood back next to Lucinda.

"Thank you, Gary. Sorry for just turning up. I did text Laura but didn't wait for a response, just went into autopilot and walked." I shuffled on the spot.

"Don't be silly. You don't need an invite," Lucinda said.

I smiled at them and made my way upstairs.

I walked down the landing and into Laura's room. As soon as she saw me, she leapt off her bed and ran towards me, knocking me flying. We both laughed as she lay on top of me. She rolled off and we just lay next to each other, laughing. Oh, it was so good to laugh; I mean, really laugh. We both got up and sat on her bed.

"How are you doing? And don't sugarcoat it," Laura said.

"Yeah. Okay. Each day is getting easier. Carter has finally stopped texting and calling, so that's helping, I suppose." I felt a lump in my throat, tears slowly starting to fill my eyes. "But it is what it is. It wasn't meant to be." I ran my fingers under my eyes and sniffed. "I'm so sorry to bum you out. You've just got back from St Lucia, and here I am, crying over another failed relationship." I put my head in my hands to try and calm myself down. I really didn't want to lose it in front of Laura, not today.

I felt her scoot over to my side. She held me so tight and kissed my hair. "Let it all out. You'll feel so much better," she whispered to me. She let me go and held my hand. "One day at a time, yeah?"

I gave my eyes one more wipe and smiled at Laura. "Right, okay. So, come on, tell me about St Lucia."

I listened to her as she reminisced about their honeymoon. I would love to go St Lucia; it sounded like heaven. The clear, crystal blue water and the white sandy beaches. If I closed my eyes, I could almost imagine I was there.

"Oh, Laura, it sounds amazing. I am so jealous! You look beautiful. You're glowing." She really was beautiful.

Lucinda interrupted us with two cups of tea. Just what I needed.

"Thanks, Mum!" Laura shouted out as Lucinda walked out of her bedroom.

"So, how is married life treating you?"

She side eyed me then tutted. "No different, if I'm honest. It was lovely for the first few days, but before you know it, you're back in your routine and they're annoying the fuck out of you." She nudged me and winked. She was so harsh to Tyler sometimes.

"Oh, don't be like that, Lau! You love him."

"Of course I love him. He's my everything. I could never see myself with anyone else, but yes, he does annoy me, same as I annoy him." She stared at me "I love the man with all my heart, but you know what they're like, they always annoy you! But, you wouldn't want anyone else annoying you more than the man you love, right?" She stifled a smile.

I did know what she meant. I swallowed hard to stop that poxy lump coming back up my throat. Why did this have to happen? Why couldn't we get our happy ever after?

She held my hand. "I'm sorry, Frey Frey."

I laughed, holding back choked tears. "For what? You haven't done anything wrong. I feel so incomplete without him, Laura."

I couldn't stop them; the tears started to flow. I wiped my eyes, looked at my hands, and sighed. I now had black mascara smudged all over my hands. I must have looked like a fucking panda. Laura slid off the bed and grabbed some make-up remover wipes from her dresser. She sat next to me and took a wipe, softly wiping my smudged mascara and tear stains from my eyes. She then wiped them over my hands.

"There. Panda eyes gone." She smiled at me. We sat in silence. I had nothing else to say on the matter, and she mirrored me.

It didn't matter how much I replayed the scenario over in my head, it didn't change anything. Carter left, I didn't follow. Carter contacted me, I didn't contact him back. He tried, I didn't.

We sat in silence, watching TV. I don't think Laura wanted to hear any more on Carter. I just felt like I was bogging her down after her happy high.

"Fancy ordering a pizza?" she asked.

I looked at her. "You read my mind." I elbowed her and smiled.

Half an hour later, we were sitting cross-legged on her bed, watching *Sex and The City,* indulging in pizza. Oh, we loved Domino's.

Just as we finished our pizza, Laura's phone rang. It was Tyler. She slid off the bed and into the bathroom to talk to him. I closed the pizza box and put it on the sideboard in her room then got myself comfortable back on her bed. Laura came back in with a furrowed brow.

"Hey. Everything okay?"

She nodded. "Tyler won't be back tonight. The issue at work is bigger than they thought so he wants to get it sorted. He promised he would be back by tomorrow mid-morning." She shrugged. "Want a sleepover?"

"Oh, yes!" I nodded.

She lent me some PJs to save me walking back home again. I needed this. I quickly went into the bathroom to freshen up and get changed. I came out of the bathroom and Laura was nowhere to be seen. I checked my phone; another message from Ethan:

Hey Freya, I am thinking of coming to see you at the weekend — that ok? Let me know, Ethan X

I smiled. Bless him. It would be nice to see him; he always cheered me up. He had a new girlfriend; the waitress I embarrassed him in front of a few months ago. I was glad he met someone.

I was distracted by Laura when I heard clinking. She had a big bottle of wine in her hand and two glasses. I wasn't sure whether alcohol in my emotional state was the right thing. Before I could think any more, Laura handed me a cold glass of rosé. It slid so smoothly down my throat. Oh, it was so good.

Lucinda appeared with crisps and sweets and perched herself on the end of the bed. "It's so nice that you two are still friends. I still remember all the sleepovers you had as kids. Now look at you. Both twenty-nine this year and still inseparable." She smiled. "Have fun, girls. Try and get some sleep." She winked at us and walked out the door.

"I still can't believe you're married, Laura – actually married!" I grabbed her hand, making her nearly spill her wine as I admired her rings. They were so pretty. She had a two-carat solitaire ring with diamonds down each side of the band. Her wedding band was the same thickness as her engagement ring, again, full of diamonds. They sparkled under the light. I sighed. "Oh, Lau. I'm still so happy for you and Tyler. I love you both so much." I wrapped my arm around her neck and cuddled her.

"We love you too, Frey Frey." She giggled.

We sat snuggled into each other, making our way through the *Sex and The City* boxset.

"So, Ethan text me." She raised her eyebrows at me and I shook my head. "Anyway, he has a girlfriend now, but he said he would like to come down and see me."

She gave me the look. "Do you think that's a wise idea? Him coming to see you? What if emotions get in the way, or you know..." She shook her wine glass. "...Alcohol?" I asked as I reached for the bottle of wine and poured her another glass, and she continued "What if you do something you regret?"

I rolled my eyes at her. "I won't be doing anything. He is with someone, he is just my friend, and I think it's nice that he wants to come and see me, to make sure I'm okay. Anyway, I haven't text him back yet, so he may not even come down."

She just shrugged and grabbed the big bag of Doritos. "Crisp?" she asked, shoving them under my nose.

I took a handful and thought about what Laura said.

Was she right? Could anything happen? I shook my head. I would sleep on it and text him back in the morning. I was just glad to be with Laura, in our hometown.

I was starting working from home the next week. I had four days left of quiet time. It was good that I didn't have to go back into the office to see everyone. One of the messages that Carter sent me was to say he had set up everything for me to work from home for as long as needed. He also sent me some job openings coming up at CHP that he put me forward for. I still didn't know what I wanted to do, but I was looking forward to getting back into work – it would help keep me focused and my mind off Carter. Laura was on her phone texting Tyler. I really wanted to pick my phone up and text Carter, just to see how he was. To see how he was coping. I slowly reached over but stopped myself.

Instead, I text Ethan, telling him that I couldn't wait to see him and for him to let me know what time his train would be getting in. I put my phone back down and stared at the ceiling, again, my thoughts going back to Carter. I started thinking about his beautiful sage eyes, his light freckles across his nose and cheeks, his tousled messy brown hair, his tanned skin glistening, his six-pack, and his lips. I missed his lips, their soft kisses on mine. The thought made me shiver, and my heart hurt.

I missed him.

So much.

CHAPTER TWO

I woke the next morning and Laura was still asleep. I rolled over and looked at the clock next to me; eight a.m. I felt so rested. For the first time in the last couple of weeks, I felt good. The amazing night's sleep helped. I wasn't sure if it was the full belly from the pizza and wine, or sleeping next to Laura, but whatever it was, it certainly helped. I slid out of bed as delicately as I could and headed for the bathroom. I hopped into the double glass boxed shower. The water pressure was so much better than mine. I washed my hair and let the water take over me. I stepped out and wrapped myself up in the fluffy towels. My towels didn't feel like that. *I really must ask Mum how to get my towels like that.*

I decided I was going to go into town and do a little shop, ready for Ethan's visit. I needed some new make-up; not that I was trying to impress Ethan, but I didn't want him to look at me and realize how much of a state I was. I knew he was happy with what's her name, but I wanted to look good. Was that wrong of me?

I left the bathroom, walked into the spare room, and rummaged through Laura's wardrobe. I pulled out a chiffon vest top and pulled my River Island jeans on. I walked back into Laura's room to grab the hairdryer when I noticed Laura was awake. "Morning, sleeping beauty." "Morning." She groaned. She was not a morning person.

"I didn't wake you, did I? I was just coming to get the hairdryer so I could finish getting ready in the spare room."

She rolled over. "No, you didn't wake me. Tyler did. Calling to tell me he's getting the train back this morning."

I smiled at her. "Oh, lovely. I was going to ask if you wanted to come into town with me. I need some new make-up, but I suppose you'll stay home with Tyler?" I asked with hesitation. "Of course I'll come! Tyler won't be here 'til about one-ish, so it will be nice to get out and help you with make-up." She smirked.

"Oh, stop it. I'm not that bad!" I smirked then dodged the pillow she threw at me. "Go get ready, Mrs Smythe!"

I finished drying my hair and tousled it; I couldn't be bothered to straighten it. It was warm, but I wasn't braving getting my legs out, plus, I hadn't shaved my legs since Carter left. No need to. I sat on Laura's bed while I waited for her to get ready. I scrolled through my phone, but nothing exciting was happening. I decided to put myself to good use and make her bed. Half an hour later, Laura appeared, her blonde hair glossy and full of bouncy curls, her skin glowing. She was wearing a delicate lemon summer

17

dress with silver sandals. "Ready?" She smiled.

"Yes, I am. Let's go."

We made our way down Lucinda and Gary's sweeping staircase and into their large, light hallway. I had one more look at myself in their gorgeous, gold, ornate mirror. I didn't look too bad for a girl who had had her heart broken two weeks ago. I was finally getting my glow back.

Lucinda appeared from the kitchen. "Where are you two off to?" she asked.

"Just into town. Freya needs some new make-up and I'm going to help her." She beamed at me. "Ethan is coming down for the weekend, so she wants to make sure she looks decent." She nudged into me and poked her tongue out.

"I just want to look normal and not so dull, because that's how I feel!" I snorted.

She nodded sarcastically. "Yeah, yeah, and he's hot and now off the market also." She elbowed me.

Honestly, that woman. "Okay, okay, enough. Can we go? Lucinda, thank you for having me." Lucinda embraced me and gave me a kiss on the cheek. "You are always welcome, Freya, you know that."

I smiled at her. Laura gave her mum a kiss on the cheek. "Oh, Mum, Tyler is due back here about one. See you soon. Love ya." She waved goodbye to her mum as we left the house.

I text my mum, letting her know that we were heading into town to get some bits I needed, and also to tell her that

Ethan was coming down tomorrow and staying until Sunday.

Laura unlocked her dad's car.

"You're taking your dad's Porsche? I thought we were going on the bus."

She snorted. "No, darling. I'm taking the car. You're more than welcome to become a bus wanker, but I am taking the Porsche. Are you getting in or not?"

I threw my arms down by my sides. "Of course I'm getting in." I slid into the passenger side anxiously.

As she turned the ignition, the engine roared. I felt a pang shoot through my stomach. It reminded me of Carter's Maserati. I quickly shook that thought away.

"So, are you looking forward to seeing Mr Smythe?" I teased. I looked over at her.

She stared at me then shrugged. "Mmm, I suppose. It's been nice having a day without him after spending two solid weeks with him, but I am looking forward to getting back to our routine."

She annoys me. She has this wonderful man who would do anything for her, yet she is so harsh. I suppose they have been together for years, but I never got enough of Carter; I felt like we didn't spend enough time together.

She pulled me from my thoughts. "Anyway, what do you think you're going to do about the whole work situation? Are you staying at Cole Enterprises or are you going to move on?"

I knotted my fingers and sighed. "I haven't really thought about it, to be honest. I'm due to work from home from Monday, so I may just do that until something comes up. I don't think I can stay working under Carter. I'll never get over him if I stay there."

Laura squeezed my hand. "It will happen in its own time, babe."

I nodded. "I know. I know."

Laura pulled into the underground car park. The main town was about half an hour away. I picked my wonderful tatty bag up out of the footwell and stepped out of the car. Laura was faffing about with her hair and topping up her lipstick. I rolled my eyes and pulled my sunglasses down off my head. She finally got her arse out of the car and slammed the door "Where first, Frey Frey?"

I just stared at her. "Do I look like I know where to get decent make-up from?" I scoffed at her.

She shook her head. "You are useless, woman." She laughed.

We walked towards a big department store and through the revolving doors; the smell of perfume hit me as I walked in. High gloss tiles and counters upon counters, all selling different beauty items. I felt overwhelmed. Who knew there was such a choice for make-up? I looked at Laura, and she could tell I was completely out of my comfort zone. She smiled at me and linked her arm in mine as we headed towards the make-up counters. Already, I was racking up a bill in my head that I really couldn't afford.

"Erm, what takes your fancy?" she asked me with an awkward smile.

I felt like a deer in headlights. "Errr…" I looked around. "Let's go over to this one. This one looks good." I nodded towards MAC.

I was looking through the shelves and drawers with not a clue what I wanted. I looked behind me for Laura, but I couldn't see her. She had obviously seen something else she liked the look of. I went back to looking for something, but I really didn't know what I needed.

"Hello. Can I help you?" I looked up and saw a beautiful, pristine sales assistant beaming at me. Her pearly, straight teeth, her glistening eyes and illuminated skin. Her short hair sat perfectly on her shoulders.

"Yes. Yes, I need help." I smiled weakly at her.

She laughed. "Perfect. Okay, so what are you looking for?"

I looked back at the counters. "I don't know. My friend told me I need some new make-up, and yours was the first counter I came to." I blushed at my unfamiliarity. "I don't wear a lot of make-up, you see. My old friend, Ethan, is coming down for the weekend and, well, I thought it would be nice to have some new make-up and a new look maybe."

I realised I had just divulged way too much information – a simple 'I need a new look' would have sufficed. I shook my head.

"Say no more. Let's see what we can find, then I can do a makeover on you with the products that we've chosen and then, if you're happy, you can purchase them," she said, still with her beaming, perfect smile.

How does her jaw not hurt? Surely it's not possible to smile that much? I looked at her name tag. 'Amy'. I scoffed. Maybe this was a bad omen, given my history. Amy ushered me over to her little black stool in front of a big illuminated mirror. *Oh, God. Is this how I look? I need more than make-up to solve this.* I watched Amy potter around her counter, picking all sorts of products up. I pulled my phone out of my bag and checked to see if Laura had messaged. *Where the bloody hell is she?* I dropped her a quick message to see if she was okay. I put my phone on the little shelf in front of the mirror.

Amy walked back over to me. "Okay," she said, smiling – obviously. "I have gone for a very light feel foundation, but a perfect match for your olive skin, a light pink blusher, bronzing powder sheer coverage, highlighter, mascara, and a light pink lipstick and lip pencil." She looked like an excited schoolgirl. I didn't feel the same. She turned my chair around to face her, clipped my hair out of my face, and applied some clear product. She could obviously read my mind. "It's primer, hun." She gave a little smile and continued her makeover.

While Amy was well in her flow of my makeover, I heard my phone beep. I opened my eyes and held my finger up to her for her to stop. "Sorry. Give me two seconds." I spun around on my chair and picked up my phone; it was Laura.

Hey, I'm fine. I wasn't feeling very well so been in the loos. I have just come to get some water, you still at MAC?

I typed a quick reply back.

Oh shit, why didn't you call me!!!! Yes, still at MAC, don't think I will be leaving just yet. Make sure you come straight here ok?

Oh, that woman. I hoped she got back sooner rather than later.

While I was sitting there, I closed my eyes and tried to relax. Amy said she would be working on my base and face make-up first, then would move onto my eyes after. I took the moment to reflect on the last few weeks and how quickly everything had changed. All of a sudden, that pang hit my stomach and my heart at the same time.

Then there was Carter. There, in my mind. I remembered every little detail about him. His tousled, mousy hair, his light freckles across his nose and cheeks, his smouldering sage green eyes that glistened whenever he looked at me, and his beautiful, perfect smile.

I remembered our first night, when we were sitting in the car on our way home from the restaurant. I felt like I could feel him, feel him moving his hand up to my face and tucking my hair behind my ear. I still remembered feeling the catch in my breath when he touched me. The whisper sent a chill down my spine as I reminisced. 'I *want to kiss you*'. I still felt the intense kiss he gave me, the feeling of wanting, the sexual chemistry between us.

My heart hurt. I felt the familiar lump in my throat. I would not cry there, not after poor Amy had put blood, sweat, and tears into my face.

Again, Amy pulled me from my memories. "I need you to open your eyes now, hun." She smiled.

I dabbed my eyes gently to make sure no stray tears had left. As I looked in the mirror, I didn't recognize the girl looking back at me. She was glowing. I just stared; no expression, no words.

My eyes were drawn to the lady walking towards me. It was Laura. Oh, wow, she did look rough.

I slid off my chair and met her. "Babe, are you sure you're okay? You look awful."

She nodded and sat in my chair. "Yeah, I'm okay. I think it was the pizza we had last night." She put her head in her hands. "I've got a thumping headache."

I looked around to ask Amy for a glass of water but she had already gone.

We had the same pizza. How could it have affected her and not me?

"Oh, Lau. I'm sorry, sweetie." I stroked her hair. "That timing, eh?"

She just groaned at me. Amy re-appeared and gave her a glass of water. She walked over to another counter and asked her colleague if she could take her chair just to finish my make-up. "Lau, I don't think I will be much longer. Are you okay to wait or do you just want to go home?"

She shook her head while sipping her water. "No, no. It's fine. I'm feeling much better."

I gave her a sympathetic look. I felt so sorry for her being unwell, especially because Tyler was on his way home.

I gave Amy an apologetic look. "I'm so sorry, Amy. This won't take much longer, will it?" I asked, looking back at Laura.

"Not much longer. I will do your eyes quite basic with a light eyeshadow and then a darker, smokier look with the eyeliner and mascara."

I nodded.

Fifteen minutes later, Laura was looking worse for wear, staring blankly into space.

"Okay, Freya. You're all done. What do you think?" Amy held a mirror up in front of me.

I couldn't believe it was me. My grey eyes stood out against the softness of the eyeshadow, but also because of the harshness of the eyeliner and mascara. My skin was glowing. The light pink blush made my cheeks look slightly bitten. The sun kissed bronzer contrasted against the blusher and gave me a healthy-looking glow. The highlighter emphasized my cheek bones and my lips looked even fuller because of the light pink lipstick and lip liner.

"Oh, Amy. Thank you. I feel amazing. Thank you so, so much." I slid off my chair and walked over to the till. Another five minutes passed while she was telling me about all the different brushes and blending sponges she had used, so obviously, I had to buy them as well. As she was putting it all through the till, I winced. "Okay, that will be £323.68 please," she said, and there was that perfect pearly white smile.

I swallowed hard. After paying for my expensive make-up, which probably would never look like the same again, I went to get Laura. As I helped her up, Amy beamed. "You have a lovely day, ladies!"

I smiled sarcastically at her. *I bet you're going to have a better day with that commission, bitch.* Must have been the name.

We walked towards the underground car park.

"You're going to have to drive, Freya. I can't drive while feeling like this."

My hands went clammy. "What? I haven't driven for months! I can't drive your dad's Porsche!"

She slapped me on the back. "Just fucking drive. Seriously, Freya," she snarled.

I put my bags in the boot and helped Laura into the car. I took a deep breath and sat next to her in the driver's side. *God help me, please*, I thought, as I started the engine.

CHAPTER THREE

After stalling the car five times and over revving the engine, when I finally thought I had the hang of it, we pulled up onto Gary and Lucinda's driveway. I had already called Lucinda on our way home to tell her that Laura wasn't feeling well.

As we pulled up, Lucinda ran down the driveway and helped Laura out of the car. "Oh, sweetie. You are so pale. Go upstairs to bed, love." She passed Laura to Gary and he slowly walked her into the house. Lucinda turned around, worry all over her face. "Thank you, Freya. This is the third turn Laura has had since they've been married. I'm worried she's picked up some tropical virus." She shook her head. "Seriously, thank you for bringing her home."

I smiled at her. "Don't be silly. I love her. Of course I would look after her. Please let me know that she's okay. Is Tyler not here yet?"

"No, love, not yet. Train delayed, apparently." She didn't look convinced.

"Give her a kiss for me. Let me know how she is tomorrow, please." I smiled. I gave Lucinda a kiss on the cheek, handed back Gary's keys, and said goodbye.

I walked slowly back to my mum and dad's house. A chill was still in the air but it felt amazing. I heard my phone beep. I swapped my newly purchased make-up into my other hand and reached around in my bag. I smiled as I saw Ethan's name on the screen.

Hey you, my train arrives at 10:34 tomorrow morning, I will jump in a taxi and meet you at your parents. I have something for you, see you tomorrow xx

He has something for me? Now I was intrigued, nervous, and excited at the same time. I walked up my mum and dad's pretty pathway and stopped to look at their cottage. It was such a beautiful place. I let myself in through the front door.

"I'm home!" I shouted.

Silence.

I looked at the time. Three fifty-three p.m. *Where could they be?* I placed the keys on the table next to the front door and slowly closed it. I put my bags down on the stairs and walked into the kitchen. There, like always, was a note:

Freya,

Me and your dad have gone for a walk to get some fresh air. Dad is feeling a bit under the weather. Lunch is in the oven if you want it.

>   *See you soon,*
>   *Love,*
>   *Mum xx*

I put the note back down on the table and made my way to the oven. I wasn't hungry, just curious. As I opened the oven, the smell hit me. *Mmm, homemade lasagne.* Before I could think about what I was doing, I pulled the dish out of the oven, picked up a fork, and sat down at the table. I read Ethan's message again while shovelling lasagne in my mouth. *He has something for me. Wouldn't it be nice if it was a semi-naked Carter in a bow?* I smirked while eating more. To be honest, I could have had Carter semi-naked in a bow, but I didn't contact him back. I left it. I put my phone down and pushed the dish away, I had eaten nearly half a lasagne and I wasn't even fucking hungry. I tutted at myself. Such a pig.

I put foil over the lasagne and slid it back in the oven then made my way upstairs. I felt sweaty and needed a shower. My face was thick with make-up. Yes, it looked nice, but it didn't feel it. I dumped my expensive make-up and brushes on the floor and made my way to the bathroom. I dropped my clothes in the laundry basket and stepped into the shower. After a good fifteen minutes of scrubbing my face, I was finally make-up free. I threw my PJs on and fell onto my bed. Oh, it felt amazing. I'd just closed my eyes when I heard the front door go. I jumped up, ran downstairs, and saw Mum and Dad walking in.

"Hey, are you okay? Dad, are you feeling okay now? I couldn't even call you because you left your mobile here." I pointed to the table. "Please, Mum, take your mobile with you," I said abruptly.

She stared at me, pressing her lips into a thin line. "For goodness sake, Freya!" she snapped. "How do you think we coped back in the days with no mobile phones? We walked around the village and stopped off to get a drink. Stop fussing, will you?" She shook her head.

I looked at my dad, and he looked worn out. "Daddy, why don't you go and lie down?"

He smiled at me. "I'm okay, love. I've just got a bit of a cold coming, I think. You know what I'm like when I'm ill. I can't look after myself." He chuckled, but I wasn't convinced. "Dad, please just go sit down. I will put the kettle on and make a cuppa." I smiled. "Mother, do you want one?"

She just nodded. She threw such strops. I was so glad they were looking after me and not rushing me to leave, but I was looking forward to heading home on Monday. Back to my flat. Back to reality. I needed to start looking for a new job when I got home. I would stay at Cole's Enterprise until I found something else that suited.

I took the teas over to Mum and Dad, and gave Dad a peck on the cheek. "Dad, I hope you haven't got what Laura has. Lucinda is worried that she's picked up some tropical virus or something." I pulled a face and shrugged.

He mirrored my face. "That isn't a tropical virus!" he shouted, and my mum shot him a look. "What you going on about?" I threw them a puzzled look.

"Nothing. I'm just saying it isn't a tropical virus."

I shook my head. "Right, okay then. I'm going upstairs to watch telly. I'm beat. Ethan's train gets in at ten thirty-four. He said he's going to get a taxi so he will just meet me here." I smiled. "Shall I set his room up before I go up?"

Mum shook her head. "No, dear. I will sort it in the morning."

"You sure?"

She smiled. "Yes, love. Now, throw your dirty washing down and I will get it washed and ironed ready for the morning. Love you."

Oh, she's back. Phew! Couldn't cope with a mother meltdown.

"Love you, Daddy. Feel better."

He blew me a kiss. "Ditto, darling."

I plugged my phone in, climbed into bed, and turned on my TV. I decided to put on *Sex and The City*; easy watching. My phone vibrated. It was Laura just letting me know that she was feeling so much better and she would call me in the morning.

I spent the whole evening watching *Sex and The City*. I looked at the time. It was nine twenty-two. I needed an early night. I needed my sleep and a clear head for Ethan in the morning. No doubt he was going to want to talk about what happened and how I was. I wasn't going to lie, every time my phone went off, I hoped it was Carter, but why would it be? He had no reason to contact me. I deleted his number. Of course, I still had his email, but I had added that onto my block list. I had been through one betrayal, I couldn't cope with anymore. I know they say if you love someone you can get through anything, but I didn't think I could. All I saw was him and her, her and Jake; the same scenarios going over and over in my head. He obviously felt something for her to want revenge on me. That was the thing that hurt the most, that he wanted me for revenge. It was always about revenge. I felt my eyes getting heavy. I left SATC on in the background; it was nice to have a bit of noise.

I had a crap night's sleep. The dreams that kept waking me shattered my heart all over again. The dream always started out like, well, a dream. Everything was perfect. Me and Carter, then all of a sudden, I felt the anxiety creeping up through my body and I woke with a jolt, sweating, heart racing, and tears. I lay in bed for a while, staring at the ceiling, playing the last few months over. Our relationship felt like a dream, like it was never meant to be. I picked up my phone and looked at the one photo I had of me and him. We were in the hotel lobby and Ava took the photo of us. He was so handsome. We looked like the perfect couple. I smiled. *Oh, Carter.* Would I have preferred to not know about it? Continue our relationship that was based on lies? But then it wouldn't have been a lie because I never would have known about it. It was bittersweet. I sighed. It was eight-thirty. Time to get up and showered and try and make myself look decent, not just for Ethan, but for myself. After um-ing and ah-ing on an outfit, I decided to go with a denim skirt and a pale pink t-shirt and, of course, my flip flops. It was warm; the sun was beaming through the windows. It was going to be a good day. I could feel it.

I sat down in front of my mirror and dried my hair; it really needed a cut. I then ran the straighteners over it, the auburn shining in the sunlight. I clipped part of my hair off my face and started rummaging through my make-up bag. I took the primer and put a little bit on my face, slowly massaging it into my skin. I then pulled the foundation brush out and applied a thin layer of foundation; already I had a glow. A bit of blush along the cheek bones and some highlighter applied, I then went onto YouTube to see how to do smoky eyes. After five failed attempts, I just decided on mascara. I then applied the light pink lipstick which matched my t-shirt and sprayed my Chanel No.5. I looked in the mirror. Okay, so it wasn't the same look the bitch had given me, but it was pretty close. Sort of.

I went downstairs to make a cup of tea to try and calm my nerves. I was feeling really anxious. Mum and Dad were pottering about in the garden. Dad had his colour back which was a relief. I looked at my phone. Ethan would be arriving any minute. The taxi ride was only five minutes away. Just as I slid my phone in the back pocket of my denim skirt, I heard a knock on the door. Oh, God. My heart started thumping; I could hear it in my ears. I swallowed hard and made my way to the door.

"Ethan!"

He dropped his bag to the floor and held his arms out. I threw my arms around him. He wrapped his arms around my waist and picked me up. "Oh, I've missed you!" I beamed at him. "It feels like it's been forever!" He put me down, smiling at me.

There it was; his beautiful, crooked smile. His hazel eyes wide with excitement, his messy blonde mop of hair hanging just above his eyes; he looked good, better than I remembered. "How you doing?" he asked me. "Are you going to let me in or are we just going to stand here on the doorstep?"

I giggled nervously. "Of course! Come in!" I put his bag on the stairs, ready to go up. We then walked into my mum and dad's living room. "Mum, Dad, this is Ethan." I smiled, looking up at him.

"Oh, Ethan. What a pleasure it is to meet you." She walked over and gave him a kiss on the cheek. Dad followed her, shook his hand, and patted him a little harder than he should have on the back. Ethan coughed in response.

"Would you like a cup of tea? Or a cold drink? I've just put some bacon on for bacon sandwiches." Mum beamed at him.

He blushed and smiled back at her. "Thank you, Mrs Greene. That would be lovely. I'm starving."

She smiled. "Please, it's Rose."

We sat down at the dining room table while Mum pottered in the kitchen and Dad disappeared back into the garden.

"So, where is that little tiger of yours?" Ethan elbowed me and winked.

"Tilly? She's upstairs. She sleeps in Mum and Dad's room now. I'm worried about how she will react when we go home on Monday," I said, looking down at the table.

"She will be fine, especially once she's back with Erin," he teased.

"How are things with you and..." I trailed off.

"Isabella. Her name is Isabella." He laughed. "Things are going really well. It's only been a month or so, but it's good. We're enjoying each other's company."

My mum came over and handed us our teas and bacon sandwiches. Ethan didn't waste time before tucking in, making noises as he enjoyed his first bite.

I smiled at him then nodded. "That's nice." I wrapped my hands around my mug. "I'm glad you've found someone, Ethan." I smiled weakly at him, and he gave me a sympathetic smile back.

"Oh, before I forget, I have something for you." My heart started thumping again. I watched him get up and walk over to his bag. I tapped my fingers on the table anxiously. He returned with a white envelope with my name on it. "Here." He held out the envelope. "It's for you. From Carter."

Just hearing his name sent shivers up my spine. I didn't know what to do. Did I want to read it? Should I just burn it? How did Ethan get this? Were he and Carter friends? I had all those questions going around in my head, but I couldn't get the words out. I just continued to look at the envelope, puzzled, my eyes darting back and forth across my handwritten name on the front.

"Your mum is going to take me upstairs and show me to my room. You haven't got to open it now, or open it at all." He sighed. "But I said I would give it to you. He deserves to be heard, Freya. You owe him that." He kissed me on the head before disappearing upstairs with my mum. I leaned the letter up against the vase on the middle of the table and continued to stare at it. My eyes were burning. I was intrigued yet scared.

No rush, Freya. Take all the time you need.

CHAPTER FOUR

After what felt like a lifetime, I slowly lifted the seal on the back of the envelope. I ran my finger underneath, heart beating, thumping in my chest. I slowly took the handwritten letter out and left it folded on the table, just for a minute, while I gathered my thoughts. Fifteen minutes later, the letter was still sitting there, unfolded, in the middle of the table. I sat back down with my cup of tea. Ethan was sitting with Dad in the living room, chatting away as if they had known each other for years. Mum was happily doing the washing, casually side-eyeing me every few minutes. I took a mouthful of tea, my stomach in knots. They say tea makes everything better, but I think the only thing to make this better is straight vodka. *Stop being a wimp. Open the letter.*

Right. It was now or never. I could either open the letter and read it, or take it over to the oven hob and burn it. I picked the letter up and slowly walked towards the hob, pushing the gas knob down, waiting to ignite it in blue flames when a voice distracted me.

"Do you really want to do that?" I looked over at Ethan and sighed. He stood next to me and took my hand away. "Freya, you know how I felt about Mr Suit," he said, slowly trailing off. "Yeah. You thought he was a dick," I muttered.

He ignored my comment and carried on. "But he came to see me. When everything happened, he was really upset. Said you wouldn't answer his calls or messages." He gave me a sympathetic smile. "He misses you Freya." He held my hand and ran his thumb along my knuckles. I walked back over to the table and sat down, letter still firmly in my hand. Ethan followed and took a seat next to me.

"So, are you two friends now? Did you bond over beers?" I asked sarcastically.

He shook his head. "I wouldn't say friends, but, we get along better now." He shrugged.

I bit my lip and looked up at him. "What he did was out of order! He only wanted to be with me for revenge!" I could feel myself getting worked up. "He *was* a dick, Ethan. What he did was uncalled for. Especially when he knew what I had been through before with Jake!"

I wasn't sure why I was shouting at Ethan, but maybe this was what I needed. I needed to get angry. I put my head in my hands. "Why didn't I choose you?" I said quietly, looking up at him through my bloodshot eyes, waiting for his answer.

He took my hands away from my face and placed them

on the table, smothering them with his. "Because we were never meant to be, babe. You know that."

I nodded, letting out silent tears. I was angry, upset, hurt, and confused. We sat in silence for a few minutes, both staring at the letter.

"Just read it. Maybe it's the closure you need," he suggested. "I'm going to call Isabella. I won't be long."

Isabella? I thought, then remembered that was his girlfriend; the waitress who I fully embarrassed myself and him in front of. I was such a knob. I watched him pacing up and down, smiling while on the phone. He looked happy. I missed being happy. I groaned. I picked the letter up and slowly unfolded it. Maybe Ethan was right. Maybe this was the closure I needed.

I took a deep breath and began to read

Freya,

I am sorry for this letter, but this is the only way I knew you would listen, especially when Ethan gave it to you.

I know I have said this over and over again in the text messages and voicemails, but I really am sorry. Yes, my intention was to get revenge, but as soon as I saw your beautiful face, that revenge left. I fell in love with you. I have never felt this way about anyone.

Let me fill you in on what happened that has led us to this:

Amy was, in fact, one of my girls. there was something about her that made me think I wanted more. she was unlike the other girls. I started to develop feelings for her, but she was never interested in me like that. it was all about the money with her. I am laughing to myself as I'm writing this as I was stupid enough to not realise her ways at the time. She started acting weird, missing her shifts. I started to get suspicious, so I had someone follow her which led me to Jake. It seemed that Amy and Jake had been having an affair for a while, which you knew. (I am not a stalker, I promise, I just have contacts, you know... if ever needed) I was so angry with everything that I started looking into Jake's life. that's when I came across you. beautiful you. I thought if I started something with you, Jake would feel how I felt when I found out about him and Amy. But he didn't. I felt the hurt, the heartbreak, the loss. I should have told you about this on our first date, but then again, at the time I didn't see myself falling for you as hard as I did.

I know me explaining it probably doesn't make it any better, but I just wanted you to know my reasons.

I love you Freya, with all my heart. Even though I feel like I have no right to love you, because it was me who chose to walk away from you when I could have stayed there and tried to make this right.

I feel like I have no right to miss you, even though I do. my heart feels like it's been shattered into a thousand pieces. I feel empty without you.

Freya, I still love you, more than you will ever know.

I wish I could see you, smell you, hear your voice, and kiss you one more time, because I would make sure I remembered every single detail.

I hope you get to read this.

I haven't stopped thinking about you.

Take all the time you need with work. if you want to leave I will understand.

You honestly were my everything, Freya. I was stupid to throw it away over something that I realize meant nothing to me.

No one will ever take your place. I promise.

Love you always
Carter X

I screwed my nose up at the letter. I wasn't sure what to think of it. I pushed it away and sighed. Ethan appeared in the walkway.

"Hey, what are you thinking?" he asked.

I tapped my fingers on the table. "I really don't know. Not sure if it's helped or made the situation worse." I shrugged.

He walked over and sat down next to me. "Look, Freya, if it makes you feel any better, he looked fucking awful." I stared at him. "His eyes were dark, he hadn't shaved in days. He looked washed out and tired."

41

I looked back at the letter and my heart sank. I took a deep breath and exhaled. "Well, at least he explained why he did what he did," I mumbled. "Not that it makes it any better, but at least I have an explanation." I smiled weakly. "Plus, it makes me feel a bit better that he feels like shit too."

Ethan ran his hand through his hair. "So, what are you going to do now?"

I took a big mouthful of my now cold tea. "Nothing. He's explained himself. It doesn't change anything. I'm not going to call him because I read his letter." Ethan blew his cheeks up and widened his eyes. "What? Do you think I should call him?"

"I'm not telling you to do anything, but I think the least you can do is drop him a message or a call."

I threw him a dirty look. "Can't," I said bluntly. "Don't have his number." I crossed my arms and looked away.

"I have it," he said, smiling and waving his phone in front of my face. "Freya, I don't know what you're trying to prove. You both clearly love each other, yet you're being too fucking stubborn to do anything about it!"

"You hated him a few weeks ago!" I shouted.

He gritted his teeth in frustration. "I didn't hate him. Hate is a strong word. I just didn't like him, but, I've got to know him, and I know how happy you both made each other and how much you really love each other. Don't go through life regretting this. Just drop him a message. Just to let him know you've read it." He passed his phone across the table and I looked up at him, at his beautiful hazel eyes, that lovely, crooked smile spreading across his face. "Please, Freya."

I let out a groan. "Fine! Give me your phone!" I snapped. He had a stupid grin on his face as he happily slid the phone closer to me.

Oh, surprise, surprise; a new message to Carter was already open. He wasn't stupid. He had deleted all the messages from them both. I shook my head.

I stared at the phone for a few minutes before typing a quick message:

It's Freya, I got your letter from Ethan. Thanks for clearing that up.

I hit send before Ethan could moan at me for what I had written. There was nothing wrong with it; that was all I had to say. Plus, I was stubborn. I never gave in.

"Anyway," Ethan said, standing from the kitchen chair. "Fancy the pub?" He gave me a wink. I nodded and smiled back at him. He looked so relaxed. He wore a navy Ralph Lauren polo shirt, skinny blue jeans, and white Converse. "Come on then." He reached up and stretched, his shirt lifting up to his hips. I could see his golden skin and six pack peeking out of the bottom. My mouth went dry; he did have a good body.

I quickly stood up. "Give me two minutes. Just going to freshen up." I smiled at him as I ran out of the kitchen and up the stairs. I walked into my bedroom and looked at my make-up; still good. I topped my lipstick up and made sure I had no lipstick on my teeth. I sprayed some more perfume and gave my auburn hair a quick brush. I took one last look at my outfit and pulled my denim skirt up slightly. I went back downstairs to find Ethan already waiting at the front door with my bag.

"Ready?" He flashed me that smile.

I took my bag from him and nodded as I walked out the door, Ethan following close behind me.

We sat down at our local pub in the village. This was where Carter saw Jake. I shook away the memories; not tonight. I was not ruining my weekend with Ethan. We were sitting at the back of the village pub; it was light and airy, but still had the traditional pub smell. I finally felt like I was starting to be myself again. Maybe the letter helped me get closure. Ethan disappeared to the bar to get some drinks, and I took the opportunity to check my phone and drop Laura a quick message to see how she was feeling. I silenced my phone and put it face down on the table. Ethan appeared with a bottle of Bud and a bottle of ice cold Sauvignon Blanc. He placed the ice bucket next to me, opened the wine, and slowly poured me a large glass.

"Thank you." I smiled at him, and he smiled back and nodded at me.

He sat down and held his bottle up. "Fancy getting drunk?" He smirked at me.

I really didn't know if this was a good idea or not, but

to be honest, I didn't care.

Three glasses down already, Ethan came wandering back with more beers. I just realised I hadn't eaten; I was hungry. I needed to eat, otherwise I would be sick.

"Hey, I'm going to order some chips. Want some?"

His eyes looked me up and down as I stood up. He began to say something but bit his tongue instead. "Sure!"

I walked over to the till to order.

"Hey, Freya. How you doing?" Tristan asked. Tristan was the pub manager. He had worked there just under six years. He was tall with black hair, very slim, with deep brown eyes. They almost looked black.

"Hey, Tristan! I'm doing great! Thanks for asking!" I sounded too enthusiastic. "How about you? How's the wife and kids?" I smiled at him.

"All good my end. Who's the fella you're with? Boyfriend?"

I snorted and laughed. "Ha! No, that's Ethan. We're good friends. He has a girlfriend. He just came to visit."

Tristan just nodded and smirked. "What can I get you?" I tried to see how much wine I had left but couldn't see the bottle and I couldn't get Ethan's attention. "Erm, can I have another bottle of the Sauvignon please, and two bowls of chips?"

He tapped on his computer screen and ripped off the receipt. "All done. It's on your tab."

I thanked him and walked back to the table with a fresh

bottle of wine; it really was going to be a messy night. "Fancy some shots after this?" I grinned at him.

CHAPTER FIVE

We stumbled out of the pub, and I was holding onto Ethan for dear life. It was so quiet. We staggered home through the cobbled streets.

"Thank you for a fun evening." I beamed at him.

"You're welcome." He winked at me. He made my tummy flutter. Just as we were approaching my mum and dad's house, Ethan lost his footing and took me down with him. He landed face down on the cobbles and I ended up on top of him.

I burst out laughing. "Oh my God, Ethan. Are you okay?" I asked through giggles. I tried to stop, but the more I tried, the more I laughed. Ethan rolled over. I went to stand up when he pulled me back down on top of him.

"I'm fine." He smirked.

"You've grazed your face," I said through a stifled laugh.

"Fuck's sake," he said, before throwing his head back and chuckling. We must have stayed there for a good fifteen minutes, laughing and replaying it over and over. Once we calmed down and actually realised the severity of the situation, Ethan winced as he moved slightly. "Can we just lay here for a minute? I think I've broken a rib."

I laughed at him. "You want to stay lying on a cobbled path because you think you've broken your rib? Let me look at it." I slowly moved his polo shirt up. He winced as I got to his ribs. "Shit, sorry." His beautiful skin glowed in the street lights. I ran my hand up his belly; I could feel his six pack. I slowly ran my hand over his ribs. Shit, they were bruised. "Yeah, we might have to take a trip to the hospital in morning."

He pushed his top down. "I'll be fine."

I shook my head at him. I slowly ran my hand through his curly blonde hair and looked at the graze on his forehead. Before I could register what I was doing, I leaned down and kissed his forehead then trailed down to his nose. "Sorry," I muttered. I stood up and pulled my skirt down and brushed myself off. Ethan was just staring at me.

He slowly got up and stood in front of me. "What was that about?" he asked.

"I don't know." I knotted my fingers and looked down. "I just forgot myself for a minute." I smiled at him. "Come on. Let's get you home."

We walked slowly in silence up my mum and dad's footpath, and I let us in. Ethan tripped over the threshold and grabbed me to stop himself falling.

"Seriously, what is wrong with you?" I burst out laughing, and he laughed with me.

"Too much to drink, that's what," he whispered.

I sat on the stairs and threw my flip flops by the front door. "I'm going to get some water. Want some?" I asked.

"Yes, please. I'm just going to sit here a minute." He winced as he sat down.

I walked into the kitchen, hitting my hip on the sideboard in the living room. "Shit!" I giggled. *Shh, Freya*, I told myself. I was banging around the cupboards until I found two glasses. I filled them up and walked back out of the kitchen over to the stairs where Ethan was still sitting. "Let's get you to bed."

We walked up the stairs together, slowly. I must have spilled my water about five times on the carpet. As we got to the top of the stairs, my dad was standing there.

"Everything okay, Freya? Sounded like we were being ransacked."

"Yeah. Sorry, Dad. I needed water and I hit my hip on the sideboard. We think Ethan might have broken his ribs so I'm just helping him to bed."

My dad shot Ethan a look. "That's not good. I'll drive you to the hospital tomorrow if-"

Ethan cut him off. "Thank you, Harry, but honestly, I think they might just be bruised."

My dad shook his head. "Let's just see how you are in the morning, son." He nodded at Ethan and kissed me on the cheek. "See you both in the morning." He disappeared back into his bedroom and shut the door.

As we shuffled down the landing, I stopped outside my bedroom. "Stay there. I just want to put my water down, otherwise I'll have nothing left." I smiled then handed his glass. I walked into my bedroom and placed my glass down on the side unit next to my bed. When I walked out of the bedroom, Ethan had disappeared. I tiptoed down to the spare room at the end of the landing. There he was, spread out like a starfish on the bed.

"You okay?" I asked.

He leaned up on his elbows. "I'm fine." He smiled at me.

"Okay, well, goodnight. Thanks for a lovely evening. I've missed you."

"Night, Freya. I've missed you too." I turned on my heel and tiptoed back into my bedroom. For some reason, I felt disappointed. Disappointed that he didn't kiss me back, but then, he did have a girlfriend. I sighed to myself. I made my way to the bathroom and splashed my face with cold water then wiped my make-up off. I went back into my bedroom and got my pyjamas out. It was quite a warm night so I decided on an oversized t-shirt. I took my t-shirt off and threw it on the floor. I undid my denim skirt and slowly slid it over my bum. As it reached my feet, I kicked it off and watched it fly through the air and land on the other side of the room. Oops.

I stopped and looked at myself in the mirror. I was wearing the lace underwear set I bought for mine and Carter's first date night. The break-up was obviously doing something in my favour; my stomach looked flatter, my legs not as thick. I turned to the side and checked myself out when I was interrupted by Ethan clearing his throat. I turned to face the door, horrified. I grabbed my t-shirt dress and held it up against me.

"Sorry, I should have knocked," he said, walking slowly into the room. "I just wanted to make sure we were okay. You know, after the little kiss incident."

I was still trying to make sure everything was covered. "Oh! Yeah! Of course, we're fine!" I over-exaggerated the *fine*.

He stood in front of me. "You look good. No need to hide in front of me." I could feel his breath on my face. I looked up at him, his hazel eyes burning into mine. I leaned up and pushed one of his floppy curls away. I stilled my breathing. He placed his hands either side of my face and slowly touched my lips with his, the kiss getting deeper, his tongue pushing and caressing my mouth.

I was so confused. I wanted this, but I didn't. He wasn't Carter. At the same time, it was so nice to feel wanted again. He let go of my face, slowly pulled the t-shirt away from my body, and dropped it to the floor. His hand rested on the small of my back as he pulled me closer to him. I ran my fingers through his curls and grabbed them as the kiss got more intense. He pulled away and started kissing down my neck, my breathing getting faster. He picked me up and moaned slightly while wincing. I wrapped my legs around him. He walked us over to my bed and sat down so I was facing him.

"Hey. Hey, stop." Miss Sensible kicked in. "What are we doing?" I pushed myself away slightly by pressing his chest.

"I don't know, Freya. Just going with the mood. You want this as much as me, don't you? You know we've wanted this from the moment we met in the furniture shop." I bit my lip. "Don't bite your lip," he said in a husky voice. He ran his hand through my hair and tugged at it. He kissed my neck, slowly trailing sweet kisses over my collarbone. I could feel him growing underneath me. I slowly lifted his t-shirt over his head, trying to do it as softly as I could so I didn't hurt him. I pushed him back gently so he fell onto the bed. I put my hands either side of him and leaned down slowly so I was just above his face, my hair falling around us. I looked at every single detail of his face; he was handsome. Before I could stop them, my thoughts turned to Carter. His beautiful sage green eyes, his strong jaw, his perfect smile and teeth with his glowing olive skin. I closed my eyes for a moment. I couldn't do this. I loved Carter. I only wanted Carter. I sat back up.

Ethan rested on his elbows. "Hey, what's wrong?" he asked, cocking his head to the side.

I shook my head. "I can't do this, Ethan. I love Carter. And, you are with, erm, I can't remember her name."

He rolled his eyes. "Isabella." He sighed. "You're right. I can't do that to her. Besides, you just said it, you love Carter. I just don't understand what's stopping you from sorting all this drama out with him." He shuffled underneath me.

I realised I was only in my underwear. I blushed and scrambled off him as quickly as I could. I picked up my t-shirt dress and quickly put it on. He was now sitting on the edge of the bed. "So, Freya, what *is* stopping you sorting it with Mr Suit?" he questioned me again.

"It's complicated," I mumbled.

Ethan shook his head. "It's only complicated because you're making it complicated. Just call him and get it sorted, otherwise he'll move on and you'll regret it. Then it will just be you and Tilly cat, unless she resides here." He shrugged at me.

Damn. I hate it when he's right.

He stood up and came to hug me. "Please, Freya. Don't let him slip away. There is only so long he will wait."

I sighed. I knew he was right. Who was to say Carter hadn't moved on already?

Ethan and I said our goodnights. He gave me a kiss on the cheek. I smiled up at him. "Goodnight, Ethan." He gave me a wink and walked out of the room.

I followed him and shut my bedroom door. I needed to

call Laura in the morning and let her know what had happened. I fell into bed, suddenly feeling sober and exhausted.

After an hour of tossing and turning, I gave up trying to sleep. My mind was racing. Did Carter still want me? Was he with anyone else? Could I forgive him? Would we be okay if we got over this? Could I forget?

I pulled my pillow from underneath me and threw it over my head. I did still love him, so, so much. I thought about him every morning when I woke up and every evening when I went to bed. Yes, he was a bit of an arsehole when we first got together, but he soon softened up. We were good together. He made me feel so alive. Every sense became stronger when I was with him. I knew he was my soulmate, but because of my stubbornness, I let him get away. The one man I truly loved.

I rolled over and looked at my phone. Just after four a.m. God, I was so tired, and so done with being awake.

I started thinking about Jake and how our relationship used to be; it was so stale. The image of those two shagging on my new rug played over in my mind. The stupid lies that came out of his mouth. '*It's not what it looks like*'. I laughed to myself. He was such a dick. I don't think we were truly happy, we just went with it because it was all we knew. We were comfortable. I always followed him wherever he wanted to go. He never wanted to listen to my hopes and dreams. He was never interested in me. I felt tears starting to fill my eyes. I was never enough for him, which hurt me. We were high school sweethearts, destined to be together forever. If he had never cheated on me with Aimee, I wouldn't have been there now. I would still have been living in my beautiful cottage, with my lovely rug and fireplace, completely oblivious to Carter. But then again, if you are truly meant to find your soulmate, would I have bumped into him eventually? I scrunched my nose up.

As I lay in bed, I felt dirty. I could still smell Ethan on me. I threw the covers back and quietly walked across to the bathroom. I turned the shower on and started undressing. I threw everything in the laundry basket. I just wanted his scent off me. I stepped into the burning hot shower and let the water wash him away. I lathered myself up and slowly washed all the suds away. The burning water was what I needed, my skin turning pink as the water hit me. I stepped out and wrapped one of Mum's famous fluffy towels around me. She would kill me in the morning, but I wasn't standing there and cleaning the glass with her squidgy. I walked back into my bedroom and dried myself. I folded the towel up and hung it on the radiator by my window. I found another big t-shirt and pulled it over my head; a familiar scent took over me. I pulled the t-shirt up to my nose and smelled it; it was Carter's. He had obviously left it when we last stayed there, when everything happened between us. The pain hit my stomach. I missed him. I got myself into bed and cuddled into my quilt. The smell was comforting and heartbreaking at the same time.

I felt my heart shatter into pieces once more.

I picked up my phone and started scrolling through it. I subconsciously clicked through the menus and ended up on the blocked list. There it was. Carter's number. I clicked unblock. Before I could register, I opened a message and clicked on his name. My fingers hovered over the keyboard for ages. I just didn't know if this was the right thing to do. After contemplating for another fifteen minutes, I typed a message, a very simple 'Hey x'.

Once it had sent, I locked my phone screen and snuggled back down into bed. I just needed to sleep.

CHAPTER SIX

"Freya, is everything okay? You've been staring at the wall for quite a while. Do you need some water?" Courtney, my assistant, asked.

I shook my head. "God, sorry, Courtney. No, I'm fine. Just had a lot on my mind this afternoon." I smiled at her. "Is there anything you need from me?"

"No. Just wanted to make sure you're okay." She smiled sweetly at me. "Would you like a coffee?"

"Yes, please. Thank you, Courtney."

She turned on her heel and walked towards the kitchen. I couldn't believe it was the beginning of September already. A whole year. I sighed. I definitely needed a coffee.

I had been working at Lornes & Hucks for four months. It wasn't far from where I used to work, so the commute wasn't too bad. I took a shot and applied for a job as an assistant editor in the publishing house after a month of returning home from Mum and Dad's, and to my surprise, I got it. I was then given Courtney as an assistant. She hadn't long been out of university and wanted to get her foot in door. I never thought I would need an assistant, being an assistant myself, but she was good at managing my diary and reminding me of deadlines. I had a lovely little office in the corner of the main office. It had big floor to ceiling windows overlooking the city. I could see the Shard and the gherkin in the distance. Courtney sat just outside of my door. The pay worked, but most of all, I enjoyed it. Courtney knocked on the door and placed a hot cup of coffee on my desk.

"Thank you," I said. Courtney just smiled at me and pulled my door to.

I got myself stuck into the four contracts which were sitting on my desk for our newly signed authors. Hopefully, one day, I would have that chance. I worked for Morgan Lornes, grandson of Arthur Lornes, co-founder of the company. Morgan was married to Evangeline Hucks, the other co-founder, Bertie Hucks', granddaughter. It seemed a little bit incestuous for my liking, but then again, who was I to judge? Both the men I loved screwed me over with the same girl. Morgan Lornes was arrogant, selfish, and hot-headed, but very easy on the eye. He had cropped black hair, olive skin, and piercing bright blue eyes. They were captivating. He reminded me of Tommy Shelby from *Peaky Blinders*. I'll be honest, he scared the living daylights out of me. I know Carter intimidated me, but Morgan intimidated me on another level. I never wanted to get on his wrong side.

Five p.m. was soon approaching. Courtney had invited me out for drinks with some of the younger assistants, but I politely declined. I had a date with Laura and a *Friends* binge.

I updated my last contract and sent them over to my editor, Carla, and copied in Morgan. I shut down my computer and picked up my Louis Vuitton Neverfull. I sighed, remembering the night Carter gave it to me. I stood up and pulled my pencil dress down as delicately as I could. I turned the computer screen off and locked my drawers. I switched my office light off and shut the door behind me, making sure I had locked it. I dropped my keys into my bag and wished Courtney goodnight. "Have a good night. Be safe."

She rolled her eyes at me while flicking her bleached blonde hair. "I will." She winked at me. I held my hand up in the air and walked to the lift. As the lift arrived, I stepped inside and checked my phone. I had a message from Laura, letting me know she would be over for seven and to have the pizza ready. I smiled as I locked my phone and dropped it back in my bag. The lift stopped on the first floor. As the doors opened, I saw Morgan. He was wearing a tailored black suit with a light blue shirt and matching tie. He smelled divine. As he stepped in, he stood in front of me, looking down at his phone.

"Evening, Freya," he said in his low voice.

He startled me. "Oh, good evening, Mr Lornes." I could

feel myself blushing.

The lift doors pinged open as we came to the ground floor. I walked slowly behind him as he walked out of the doors. As soon as I could, I sped up and walked round him. I really didn't like being in his company. I pushed through the doors and let the September breeze hit me. I closed my eyes for a moment to catch my breath. As I stood on the pavement, I decided to get a cab instead of jumping on the train; it was going to cost me but I didn't care.

After standing curbside for fifteen minutes, a cab finally stopped. Just as I went to open the door, I heard Morgan call me. "Hey, Freya. One second."

I turned around to face him. I looked over at the taxi driver and mouthed, 'one minute' to him. He started the meter.

"Hey. I need you to come away with me this weekend for work. We're heading to Paris as Jude Prior is only doing one signing and I want to be there. We then have a ten minute meeting with Jude who I'm desperate to sign and I don't want anyone else getting their hands on him. Especially City House Publishing," he said with a sneer.

I felt the panic set in. *Fuck. Oh, God. I can't go if Carter is going.* I could feel my palms getting sweaty. Before I could send myself into a full blown panic attack, Morgan brought me back round.

"Also, if you could let Courtney know tomorrow, as she will be coming along as well. We will be leaving at about six p.m. on Friday. Have a nice evening, Freya." He smiled and turned on his heel. Before I could dispute it and beg for him not to send me, he was gone. I finally got into the taxi and let out a big sigh.

"Bad day?" the taxi driver asked.

I laughed to myself. "You could say that."

I had a horrible knot in my belly. I didn't need this. I still loved Carter, of course I did, but I was over the situation. He never did text me back, so that kind of gave me the closure I needed. I sat and closed my eyes. I just wanted to shut myself away for the taxi drive home. After thirty minutes of stopping and starting traffic, I was finally outside my apartment block. I gave the taxi driver his money and slid out of the car. I was so glad to be home.

I walked in the door to be greeted by Tilly cat. She purred as she rubbed herself up against my leg. I leaned down and picked her up for a snuggle and a kiss. She was cute when she wanted to be. I still don't understand why someone would abandon her, but their loss was my gain. I didn't think I was going to get her back after I moved back to Mum and Dad's. Tilly seemed to take a shine to my mum and vice versa, but she chose me in the end. Just as I was about to call for pizza, Laura text me saying that she was feeling rough with a migraine. I sighed. I put Tilly on the kitchen worktop and called my local Chinese. After a few attempts, I finally got through. "Hello, can I place an order please?"

After tucking into my Chinese, I decided to give Laura a call. As You Magazine was CHP's sister company, she may be able to see if Carter was booked at the weekend for Jude Prior's signing.

"Hey, doll. It's me." I rolled my eyes. Of course she knew it was me. I shook my head at myself. "Are you feeling better?"

"I'm okay. The migraine is finally shifting. I'm really sorry for bailing on you. Are you okay? How's work?"

"Work is okay. Well, was okay. Morgan sprung on me tonight that we're going away on Friday evening to Paris as he wants to sign Jude Prior!" I could feel myself getting worked up again.

"Surely not. Jude is a big deal. What makes Morgan think he stands a chance, especially against CHP..." Her voice trailed off. "Oh, I see."

"So, yeah, do you know whether Jools' replacement, Gino, is going? If so, that will mean Carter will go because he likes to do his own business." I was talking so fast that I couldn't even keep up with myself.

"Slow down, babe. I will check with Rachel to see if she's heard anything since she took over your job. I will drop her a text and text you back." I took a deep breath. "It will be fine, Freya. Try not to panic. He probably won't go anyway."

"Mmm, I hope you're right. Anyway, hun, we will catch up when I'm back. I miss you."

"I miss you. Love you, Freya."

"Love you too."

I got up and disposed of my food and washed my plate. I got undressed and threw my clothes in the wash basket then stepped into the shower and stood there for about five minutes, just letting the water take over my body. After debating whether it was too much to use dry shampoo for the fourth day running, I decided to give in and wash my mane. I threw on my shorts and vest top and checked my phone; I had a message from Laura:

Spoke to Rachel. C hasn't checked in to his flight or hotel, so no, he isn't going. Try and enjoy it xx

I sighed in relief. That made things a lot easier. I dried my hair with the hairdryer then messy-bunned it. It was only half past nine, but I felt wiped. I needed to go to bed, but I also had to pack for Paris. I went through my wardrobe, trying to find suitable outfits. I needed an outfit to travel there and back, two day outfits, and a couple of nice outfits, just in case we went out. I was sure Morgan would take full advantage of his all black American Express. Oh, to be that wealthy.

I decided on a leggings-type lounge suit with an oversized sweatshirt to travel in. The weather would be similar to the UK; sunny but chilly. I packed a couple of pairs of jeans, a dungaree dress, a short leather jacket, and some casual t-shirts. I decided on one floor length dress that

I had to wear for a Christmas ball, and a skater dress. I packed my Louboutins and also my silver strappy sandals I bought for my first date with Carter. I threw some underwear in the case, along with my white and black Converse. I got my passport out and left it on top of my case along with my travel documents that Morgan sent me. I was surprised I didn't have to book our flights; it was unlike him to do it. He never did anything.

I smiled to myself. That wasn't too bad. *I might dip into my savings – nothing like treating yourself while in Paris!* I got into bed and got cosy. Tilly came and joined me and snuggled up next to me. She was like a hot water bottle. I turned my lamp off and lay there for a few moments. I wondered if Carter wasn't going away because he knew I would be there. He knew where I was working as Lornes & Hucks requested a reference from Cole's Enterprises, and he was technically my boss. I often wondered if he had moved on. I couldn't see him still being single. He was too good-looking. If he had moved on then he couldn't have loved me as much as he said he did. I'd played the scenario of bumping into him over and over again. In a way, I hoped I did see him. But, then again, if I did see him, I knew I would say 'hi' to him and leave it at that.

Paris, the city of love. Maybe I would find someone new. Maybe this trip would be the fresh start I had been waiting for. I had my new job which I loved, I still adored my flat, so all that was missing was love. I looked over at my suitcase as the warm street lights gave my room a glow. This break would be good. It was what I needed. I was grateful for Morgan at that moment. I was sure I would feel differently the next day at work when he was making me hit impossible deadlines, and sit in on meetings and take minutes. I was more a PA than an assistant, but again, it was another foot in the door. I would get to where I wanted to be, but first, I had to work for Morgan. He was an arrogant bastard though.

CHAPTER SEVEN

I woke early on Friday morning. I felt like I hadn't slept. I was tossing and turning most of the night, playing different scenarios over and over in my head. I had such an overactive imagination that, somehow, in my mind, I had convinced myself that I was definitely going to bump into Carter. I groaned as I rolled out of bed. I could so have done without work. If we weren't going to Paris then I would have definitely called in sick. I walked into my little bathroom and had a shower and brushed my teeth. I could have stayed in the shower for hours, but I just wanted to get out of the house and into the office. I took my hair out of its messy bun and let my hair fall. It had formed a slight wave. I ran my hands through the ends and added some smoothing serum. I decided on a light smoky eye look and a thin line of liquid eyeliner. I put some concealer under my eyes and dabbed lightly with my finger until it was blended in. I brushed my cheekbones with bronzer and applied a red lipstick. Bold for me. I flicked mascara over my lashes to make them thicker and longer. That would do. I didn't look too bad for someone who hadn't slept.

When I started my new job, I treated myself to some new office shoes and office wear. I decided on a cropped ankle-length pair of black high-waisted trousers that were tight around my bum and hips and then tapered just above my ankle bone. I then pulled out a black tailored wrap shirt with a beautiful V-neck line which showed just enough cleavage; it had little capped sleeves. I then chose a beautiful pair of black stiletto sandals to wear. I would be moaning later because my toes would be cold. I put on my delicate Michael Kors diamante necklace that Laura and Tyler gave me for Christmas. It complimented my outfit beautifully. I grabbed my black Neverfull bag and made sure I had everything I needed for work. I walked into the lounge and said good morning to Tilly then walked over to my kettle and switched it on. I picked up a banana out of the fruit bowl and started eating that while I was waiting for the kettle to boil. I put my banana skin into the bin and made my cup of tea.

I sat on my black leather sofa and looked around my living room; it needed a change. I just didn't know what to do with it. Maybe I would look at Pinterest to see if I could get some inspiration. It was seven forty-five. I sat quietly and gathered my thoughts while drinking my tea. I was trying to mentally prepare myself for the weekend. I knew it would be fine. I had Courtney with me so it wasn't like I was just going with Morgan. I only got on with him because I had to. I washed my cup up before having to leave. I said bye to Tilly, picked my bag up off the floor and walked towards the door. I would get my suitcase that evening before heading to the airport. I locked the behind me and pulled my phone out of my bag just to make sure I hadn't missed anything. I hadn't.

As I walked down the stairs, I saw Ethan and whatsherface coming out of his apartment. Oh, shit. I didn't need this. We did speak, but not like we did before that awkward night happened. Ethan was meant to stay another day, but he didn't. When I woke in the morning, he was just about to leave my mum and dad's. I sighed at the memory. I took a deep breath and stepped into the communal hallway. I could feel his hazel eyes burning into me.

"Hey. Long time no see. How are you?" he asked as he walked over to me with her following behind him. They did make a cute couple.

"Hey you!" I said overexcitedly. "I'm really good actually. I'm off to Paris tonight with work which will be lovely." He just smiled at me, nodding. She didn't look at me. *I wonder if she knows?* "Anyway, I've got to shoot off. Don't want to be late for work. See you around!"

I heard some muffled talk behind me but didn't look back. I jumped into my taxi and headed for the station. How bloody awkward was that? After a short train ride, I arrived at the office. It was a tall, modern, glass building. Lornes &

Hucks owned the first to the fifth floors. Their offices were all beautifully designed. Each floor had a different theme; our theme was safari animals. Not quite sure why. There were life-like statues around the floor, along with extraordinary photos of more safari animals. To be honest, when I first walked in, I thought they were hideous – but I'd grown to like them.

I buzzed myself into our office after exiting the lift and walked to my desk. I smiled and nodded as people wished me good morning and I sat behind my desk. I plopped my bag on the floor and picked up my mobile. I had a quick look; nothing. I sighed. I turned on my Mac. While I was waiting for it to load, I went into the office kitchen to make myself a cup of coffee. I checked Morgan's office as I walked past. His computer was on but he wasn't there. He was a lot easier on me in the coffee scenario than Jools was. She text me last week, checking in. We spoke occasionally. She wanted to go back to You Magazine. I was hoping she did go back. She was a hard worker and a good boss. I boiled the kettle when I heard Courtney say, "Hey, travel buddy! We're sharing a room for the weekend. Aren't you lucky?" She nudged me in the ribs.

"So lucky," I replied sarcastically.

"Let's hope today flies by so we can get drunk on the plane and hit Paris!"

I laughed at her. "We're going for work, Courtney, not a weekend piss up. As much as it would be nice to be pissed all weekend, it won't happen. You have packed appropriately, haven't you?" I raised an eyebrow at her.

She rolled her eyes at me. "Of course I have, Mother!" she said with a raised voice, annoyed. I started making mine and Morgan's coffees. "Want one?" I asked her, but she had already walked out of the kitchen. Stroppy mare.

I walked into Morgan's office and, there he was, sitting there, brows furrowed, looking at his computer. "Morning, Morgan. I've made you a coffee." I smiled at him and placed it next to his computer.

"Morning, Freya. Thank you. Are you all set for this weekend?" he asked, elbows resting on his desk, fingers knotted under his chin.

I wrapped my hands around my coffee cup. "I am, yes. I've never been to Paris, believe it or not, so it will be nice to see it."

"How about to meet the wonderful Jude Prior?" He was like a child at Christmas, his crystal blue eyes twinkling.

"Very much so." I nodded. He turned away to face his computer screen, and I took that as my cue to leave. "We've got even more of a chance to nab Jude Prior now as Mr Cole isn't going." I could hear him smiling in his voice.

I turned to face him. "Oh, is he not?"

"Didn't you know? Thought you would have known given your history with him."

Fuck.

I could have handled this two ways: been a complete

ASHLEE ROSE

diva and showed myself up, or answered him back professionally.

"I have nothing to do with Carter anymore." I nodded at him and walked out of his office as quickly as I could. I just wanted the ground to swallow me up.

I sat at my desk and got lost in my work. I just wanted the day over with. Morgan had really annoyed me. Why did he have to make a comment? I looked at the clock in my office. It was four-thirty p.m. I decided enough was enough. I saved my work and shut down my computer. I picked my bag up off the floor then locked my office door behind me. I mouthed to Courtney that I was going home to get my suitcase and I would meet her back at the office at six p.m. She put her thumbs up while carrying on her conversation on the phone.

I darted past Morgan's office; there was no way I was getting dragged back in there. I stood impatiently outside the lift, tapping my foot. After what felt like hours, the lift doors opened. I let out a sigh of relief to find an empty lift. I walked out of the main office and straight into my taxi. I greeted the taxi driver and sat back in my chair. "Time for Paris," I said quietly, in a crap attempt at a French accent.

I walked through the door and straight into my bedroom. Erin must have already picked Tilly up. I got undressed and threw on my lounge suit and oversized jumper. I slipped my chestnut Uggs on as my feet always got cold on planes. I gave myself a once over in the mirror and wiped some smudged mascara from under my eyes. I put my passport and boarding pass into my bag and lugged my suitcase out the door. I locked up and jumped back in my taxi; he'd kindly agreed to wait for me if I was happy for him to leave the meter running. The taxi driver, Paul, was a right Cockney man. He came and took my case from me and put it in the boot. I had told him all about my trip to Paris and the whole Carter situation. He was very attentive; he was also very good at telling me exactly what he would do to Morgan and Carter if he was to ever see them.

He dropped me back outside my office and helped me with my suitcase. I gave him his money and waved goodbye. I honestly felt like we had become good friends. I smiled to myself. If only all taxi drivers were like him. I saw Courtney standing outside the main doors with a massive suitcase, tapping her foot impatiently while scrolling through her phone. "Courtney, darling, we're only going for two nights. Do you really need that massive suitcase?"

She tutted at me. "Of course I do." She shook her head at my little hand luggage-sized case.

We both stood and waited for Morgan; it had just gone six.

"So are you excited or are you still worrying about bumping into Carter?" she asked.

I nibbled my bottom lip. "He isn't going, so I'm just trying to focus on that. Laura would have known because she knows the two people who took over from both my positions." I sighed. "Anyway, what's the worst that can happen? I see him, I say hi, I walk away." I shook my head at what I'd just said. "Anyway, he isn't going to be there, so it will be fine. We can focus on enjoying ourselves when we aren't being made to work for Morgan. Surely we will get some down time."

She winked at me. "We will definitely get some down time. I didn't agree to this trip to be Morgan's bitch."

"Seriously, Court. It's a work trip, not a girls' weekend. Why can't you understand that?" I laughed. "Anyway, speaking of work. Here he comes."

We both looked over to see Morgan walking down the street, pulling his suitcase along. He pushed his fingers through his thick black, swept back hair, his smile growing on his face as he got closer. He was about six feet seven, broad and toned. He had a strong jaw line that was covered in dark stubble. He was handsome. Just a handsome arsehole.

"Ladies." He nodded at us. "The car is on its way. Hopefully we can whizz through the London traffic and get to City Airport as soon as."

He turned away, pulled his phone out of his pocket, and started tapping away. I just stared at Courtney. What a weekend this was going to be. Like clockwork, his car arrived. It was a blacked-out Rolls Royce; not what I was expecting at all. Courtney's eyes lit up. She pushed past me and smiled sweetly at Morgan. I couldn't stop the expression on my face – what on Earth was she doing? He opened the door for us. I followed Courtney. Morgan's driver put our cases in the boot, along with Morgan's.

While Morgan was chatting, I eyeballed her. "Don't even think about it," I said sternly. "What?" she replied sarcastically.

"You know what," I scoffed. I sat back in my chair as Morgan joined us. I smiled at him as he shut the door.

"Ready, ladies? It's going to be a great weekend. I can feel it."

I nodded in agreement while trying to cover the messages Courtney was texting me about how she wished she could feel it. I sighed heavily, shook my head, and put my phone in my bag. I closed my eyes, wishing I was in a different place while trying to ignore Courtney's flirtatious giggles and comments towards our boss.

CHAPTER EIGHT

When we arrived at London City Airport, Morgan's driver opened our door. Morgan stepped out, did his suit jacket back up, and put his sunglasses on. He checked his Rolex then straightened his tie. I stood next to him and waited for my case. Courtney stood next to me, eyeballing me the whole time. I chose to ignore her. I thanked the driver and followed Morgan into the airport. He walked straight up to security and started chatting to one of the guards. With a quick nod of the guard's head, he opened up the barrier and let Morgan, Courtney, and me through. I was a bit shell shocked; our bags weren't checked and neither were our passports. I looked behind me at Courtney and she had the same stupid expression on her face as I did.

We were rushed through to a departure lounge; no one else was there. There were beautiful Chesterfield leather sofas, a sleek mini bar with a bartender, and a large mirrored coffee table. There were flowers all around the lounge, and fresh fruit and canapés ready to be tucked into.

I was suddenly starving.

Morgan cleared his throat. "Ladies, please, take a seat. Have some food and a drink." He smiled towards the bar. "I've just got to make a few phone calls before our flight." He gave us a wink and walked out of the lounge door.

"Let's get drunk!" Courtney screamed, jumping up and down on the spot.

"Oh, Court, honestly. Enough. You can't get drunk!"

She scowled at me. "You are such a bore."

I chose to ignore her. I was not falling out with her on this weekend. She walked over to the bar and ordered a bottle of Prosecco and one glass. She was such a child at times. She came and crashed down on the sofa opposite and gave me a sarcastic smile.

"Whatever," I mumbled under my breath. I walked slowly over to the big window on the other side of the lounge. I stood watching the world go by. All the big airplanes, still, waiting for their passengers. Last time I would have been there, Carter and I would have been going to New York. I sighed.

I walked over to the bar and sat on the stool. "Evening, Miss. What can I get you?" The barman's warm smile instantly pulled me back from my mood. He had dark brown hair, French cropped with a neatly shaven beard. He had deep blue eyes and freckles. When he smiled, he had the most amazing dimples. I felt myself melt.

"Miss? Can I get you anything?"

I smiled, embarrassed. "Yes," I whispered, and leaned over the bar. I looked at Courtney who seemed to be on Snapchat, doing poses. "Can I have a shot of tequila and a vodka and lemonade, please? That way, the child over there will think I have lemonade." I smiled up at him and slid back onto my stool.

"Certainly, Miss." He smiled back at me.

He slid the tequila over to me and put a salt pot and slice of lime next to it. I gave one quick look over at Courtney, who was texting on her phone. I licked my hand in the most ladylike way I could, put some salt there, and shot my tequila back. I licked the salt and sucked the lime. I shuddered as the sourness hit my taste buds. The barman was just staring at me.

"Sorry," I whispered. "It was needed. I've got to sit on a plane with her."

"I wasn't judging." He took my glass away and wiped the side down. I placed my elbows on the bar and watched him as he started to make my drink. *What a stress free job.* He gave me my drink and placed a straw in the glass.

"Thank you." I gave him a little smile.

"You are most welcome." He smirked before turning away.

I sat in silence for five minutes, just taking everything in and trying to prepare myself for the weekend. All of a sudden, the barman came back with a piece of paper and a pen.

77

"Sorry for being so bold, but could I have your number? Maybe we could get a drink when you're home?" His deep blue eyes were wide with hope.

I took the pen from him and slid the paper over to me.

"Of course. I would like that. I'm Freya, by the way."

"Luke."

I nodded. I scribbled down my mobile number and my name and passed it back to him.

"Thanks. Have a safe trip, Freya. I look forward to seeing you when you're home." He had a very chuffed look on his face. I blushed.

"Ditto."

I slid off my stool and picked up my vodka and lemonade then sat on the sofa opposite Courtney. She had finished her bottle already. She pulled herself off the sofa and headed to the bar. Just as she was about to order, Morgan walked back in.

"Let's go. Our plane is ready," he said, clapping and rubbing his hands together.

I got up and picked up my suitcase, downing my drink. Courtney sulked as she picked up her suitcase and stood by Morgan, giving me evils. Brat.

He started walking out of the lounge.

We walked straight out onto the tarmac and there it was; Morgan's private plane. I mean, of course he had a private plane. The man was a millionaire.

The pilot and cabin crew were standing at the bottom

of the stairs, waiting to greet him. "Evening, Mr Lornes." The pilot shook his hand and gestured for us to enter the plane. Our luggage was taken from us at the bottom of the stairs.

As I stepped onto the plane, I was handed a cold glass of champagne. I looked down the aisle and lost my breath. The interior was stunning. There were big, cream leather reclining armchairs, with marble tables either side of them. There was a plasma double the size of my TV back in the flat.

"Miss, would you like to take your seat?" a friendly male air steward asked me.

"Sure." I looked for Courtney, who was lapping this up. She was sitting opposite Morgan, obviously. I had never seen this side of her before.

I sat down in the chair just across the aisle next to Morgan. I downed my champagne and checked my phone. I had a message from my mum, telling me to have a lovely time. I typed a quick reply, thanking her and telling her I would call her when I landed in Paris. I then opened the next message and it was from Laura. I had to catch my breath. My throat had tightened. I tried clearing my throat, but I couldn't get rid of the feeling. I could feel Morgan looking at me.

"Freya, are you okay?" he asked.

I just nodded while staring at my phone, reading the message again and again.

Freya, Carter is in Paris. I have just

*found out. Stay calm, it will be fine. I'm
sorry. If I had found out sooner I would have
text you xxx*

I put my phone on airplane mode and threw it in my handbag. I called over the steward and asked for another champagne

"Freya, what's wrong?" Courtney asked.

"Erm, I just had a message I didn't want." I didn't have to say anything; she knew when I looked at her. She quickly unstrapped herself and came and sat opposite me.

"It will be okay, Freya. I'm here. I promise." She smiled at me and rubbed my knee. She wasn't big on affection so that was huge for her.

Morgan looked at us both, utterly confused. He shook his head and went back to his phone. "By the way, you don't need to put your phone on airplane mode on my jet," he said, not taking his eyes off his phone.

The steward returned and brought another glass of champagne. I smiled as I accepted it. Just as he went to walk away, Courtney called him. "We will just take the bottle with an extra glass. Thank you." She smiled at him as he nodded and walked away.

I just wanted to be in Paris and get the weekend out of the way. The steward placed the champagne in an ice bucket in between Courtney and me. She helped herself to a glass just as the other stewardess announced we were ready to take off and our flight time to Paris would be an hour and fifteen minutes. I downed my champagne and poured another glass. Courtney raised her glass to me in preparation for a toast.

"To you," she said as we clinked glasses.

I downed it.

"Another?" she asked with a smile on her face

I nodded. Sod it.

Our flight was smooth and quick. Morgan kept ordering us champagne; I think he knew what was going on but didn't want to say. We walked straight through the airport in Paris and got through as quickly as we did in London. We were standing outside the hotel for a few minutes before a blacked out 4x4 Mercedes stopped just past us. Morgan nodded at us to head towards the car. As much as I felt tipsy from all the bubbles, I was so ready for bed. It was nearly ten p.m. We got into the black Mercedes and got comfy, and Morgan followed us. For the first time on the whole trip, he actually put his phone away in his pocket.

"So, I was going to go through our plans tonight, but I'll be honest, girls, I'm wiped, and so are both of you by the looks of it."

Courtney and I looked at each other and smiled.

"Yeah, we are pretty beat." I answered for both of us.

"I will meet you in my suite for breakfast at eleven tomorrow morning. That gives you both a chance to lie in and get ready. We're meeting Jude on Sunday at one p.m.

Saturday is yours. You can do what you want on the company credit card. We fly home late afternoon on Monday – does that work for you?"

"That sounds perfect. Thank you, Morgan"

For the rest of the car journey, we all sat in silence.

We shortly arrived outside a beautiful hotel; the Park Hyatt. It was near the Vendôme, apparently. We walked into the lobby and it was truly breath-taking. Morgan walked over to the reception and checked us in while Courtney and I stood there with our mouths wide open. I felt like Julia Roberts in *Pretty Woman* when she sees Edward's penthouse suite for the first time. Morgan walked over after a few minutes and handed us a key card. We were staying in the Presidential Suite. Morgan told me he would be next door in the Impériale Suite, and if we had any problems, we were more than welcome to knock. We wished him a goodnight.

We walked into our room and squealed. It was like my flat times four. It was ridiculous.

We dropped our suitcases to the floor and unzipped. I was desperate to get out of my clothes and get my PJs on. Courtney was already undressed. She walked over to the super king bed and picked up her phone. She was chatting away, so I nipped into the bathroom and washed my face. I got into my PJs; they felt amazing. I walked out of the room and over to the bed where Courtney was already snuggled in.

"I've ordered room service. Burgers and champagne," she mumbled.

"Ohh, delicious. I'm so hungry."

"Me too. I'm so tired though. I could just sleep."

"So, are you going to text Carter?" she asked.

I eyeballed her. "No. If I see him then, you know. If I don't then, bonus, right?" I shrugged.

"Mmm, I'm not sure. I think you need to see him. Clear the air."

"Oh, Courtney, why is this so complicated? I just want to forget about it all."

"I know you do, but it's not that easy."

We were interrupted by a knock on the door. "Room service!"

"I'll get it," I said as I climbed over Courtney to get to the door. I unlocked it and a very smart gentleman stood there with silver dishes on a tray. I was so excited and so hungry. I thanked him and wheeled the trolley in. I said goodbye to the porter and shut the door.

"Oh, I didn't tip him!" I grabbed my purse and ran for the door. I opened it to see no sign of him. I looked down the other end of the hallway when something caught my eye. I froze.

I saw a glimpse of a man being led into a room by a lady. It was only a glimpse, but it looked like Carter. I knew what he looked like, how he carried himself.

I finally took myself back into the room and walked

slowly over to the bed.

"Freya, what's wrong? You look like you've seen a ghost," Courtney said, with a mouthful of burger.

"I did. I saw Carter."

"What? Are you definitely sure it was him and not a lookalike? Maybe your mind is playing games with you because you know he's here."

I turned to face her as I sat on the bed. "Maybe. I suppose it could have been. But even seeing him at the distance, I felt it was him. Like my body and soul knew it was him – does that make sense?"

Courtney nodded through another mouthful of burger. "I still think it's your imagination. Eat your burger, drink the champagne, and try not to think about it."

I nodded quietly and picked up my burger. Courtney started pouring the champagne as I took a big mouthful. Oh, it was good. After we had finished our burgers and champagne, I headed for the shower. It was nearly midnight. I needed ten minutes out before going to bed.

As always, my mind started wandering.

Who was the woman he was with? Is he with someone new now? Could he really be over me? Was it even him?

I got out of the shower with those questions going round and round my head. I slipped my shorts and t-shirt on for bed and snuggled down next to Courtney. She was already snoring, her long blonde hair fanned out on the pillow while her eyes were covered with a delicate sleep mask.

I rolled over, tucked my duvet under my face, and closed my eyes. I knew I wasn't going to sleep well, but I had to try.

CHAPTER NINE

I squinted as the sun shone through the curtains. I rolled over and looked at the time. It was just past nine a.m. I stretched. I actually didn't sleep too badly. I think the amount of champagne I consumed on the plane and in the hotel helped. Courtney was still asleep, so I decided to jump in the shower so I could wash my greasy hair. After, I stood in front of the mirror and just looked at myself. I missed my glow. My auburn hair was limp and lifeless. I just wanted the happy me back. A part of me was missing, the part that made me happy, and that was Carter. That familiar ache hit my heart again. I put my hand to my chest and formed a fist on my skin. I was interrupted by Courtney.

"Hey, would you mind leaving? I need to pee."

I shook my head and left.

I walked back into our suite and threw my clothes on. It was a warm day in Paris. I decided on Converse, a denim dungaree dress with a white tee underneath, and a faux leather jacket as there was a chill in the air. I walked over to the big dressing table and mirror and sat down on the velvet-cushioned stool. I rummaged through my beauty case and pulled out my tangle teaser and started battling through the knots in my hair. Courtney came out of the bathroom and offered to blow dry my hair for me. I smiled at her and accepted her offer to help me out. After about twenty minutes, my hair was full of bouncy curls and looked amazing.

"Thank you, Courtney. I really appreciate it."

"No problem. Now just sort your face out." She pointed at my face and pouted as she disappeared back into the bathroom. I rolled my eyes as she walked out.

I pulled my make-up out that I bought before Ethan's visit; it was running low. I applied it with the sponge and covered my under-eye bags. I applied a light dusting of bronzer to give me a healthy glow, and a small drop of highlighter. I flicked some thick black mascara to my lashes and watched as they became more emphasized. I reached for my red lipstick; I thought I would make my lips stand out against my denim dungarees. I rubbed my lips together and pouted in the mirror. At least I looked a bit more human.

Courtney emerged from the bathroom, looking like a goddess. Her long blonde hair was styled as if she had just come back from the beach with her perfect beach waves. Her make-up was flawless, her face shimmered, her eyes were smoky which made her stunning green eyes stand out.

She looked beautiful. She was wearing a denim skirt and a slogan t-shirt with a denim jacket and trainers.

We grabbed our bags, purses, and phones, and left our suite. Morgan was next door to us so at least we wouldn't get lost. As we entered the hallway of the hotel, I looked down to where I thought I saw Carter, hoping to see another glimpse, but I saw nothing. Maybe it was just my imagination.

We knocked gently on Morgan's door. He swung it open and welcomed us into his suite; it was huge. Ours was big, but his was ridiculous. He was on the phone as he ushered us through to the lounge area. Breakfast had already been ordered, and by the looks of it, he had ordered the whole menu. Courtney took no time in sitting down and helping herself. I was a little more patient. I watched Morgan while he was on the phone; he seemed agitated. I noticed his wedding band was missing as he rubbed his temples with his free hand. Maybe he was having issues with Evangeline. He forcefully cut his phone off and mumbled under his breath.

"So sorry, ladies. Just dealing with some personal issues." He cleared his throat. "I over ordered. I didn't know what you would like. Freya, tuck in before Courtney eats it all." He smirked and stifled a laugh. "Now, if you would excuse me, I'm going to get dressed. Sorry you've had to see me in my dressing gown." He walked away into the bathroom and closed the door.

I eyed Courtney stuffing scrambled eggs and bacon into her mouth, and I helped myself to some pancakes and fruit.

"What's up with Morgan?"

She shrugged at me with a mouthful of scrambled egg.

I sighed at her. "I think he has some stuff going on. Don't push it with him." I gave her a stern look.

"I'm not going to push it. Yes, I fancy him. Yes, I want him, but I'm not desperate!"

We sat in silence for the rest of the time while we waited for Morgan to come out of the bathroom. Half an hour later, he appeared. His black hair that was long on top and shaved round the side was slicked back, his piercing blue eyes glistening as the sun rays hit them. His strong jaw was tense. He was wearing a navy suit with a crisp white shirt underneath, with the top button undone. As he walked into the lounge area, he was fiddling with his cufflinks. Courtney had to practically scoop her mouth off the floor; she had it bad for him. To be honest, I felt like I had it bad for him too. He looked different. He was such a good-looking man, but he knew it, and that made him even sexier. As he sat at the table next to me, the smell of his cologne hit me. He smelled good.

"I apologize for making you both wait. Enjoying breakfast?" he asked with a smile.

"It's delicious. Thank you for ordering," I replied. Courtney was just staring at him and seemed to have lost the ability to speak. We sat in silence for a few minutes while he sorted himself out a plate of food.

"Sorry if this is out of line, Morgan, but you seemed tense when we walked in. Is everything okay? Is there anything we can do to help?" I asked, concerned.

I was nervous. He looked vulnerable. I would never normally have asked him anything like that, but for some reason, that day felt different. He cleared his throat.

"It's fine, Freya. Just some issues with Evangeline." He pressed his lips into a thin line and fiddled with his cufflinks again

"I'm sorry to hear that," I said sympathetically and smiled. He mirrored me and smiled back.

Once we'd finished our breakfast, a young man entered the room and cleared the table. Morgan gave him a tip and sent him on his way.

"So, let's go through our itinerary," he muttered. I pulled out my notepad and pen, ready to make note of times and places we needed to be.

"Today is a free day, until dinner tonight. We're expected to meet with some of the other publishers and Jude's representatives before our meeting on Sunday. Dinner is at seven p.m. at Le Cinq. We will meet in the lobby at six-thirty and we will go together. Dress code is formal. Like I said, take my business card and buy yourselves a new outfit tonight, and anything else you may need."

I swallowed. Could this mean Carter would be there?

My palms started sweating; I felt like I couldn't catch my breath. I stood up and walked over to the mini bar in Morgan's suite and helped myself to a glass of water.

"Are you okay, Freya?" Morgan asked.

I nodded and stuck my thumb up while smiling sarcastically before going back to my water. I sat back down so we could resume the meeting.

"Okay, then on Sunday, we're meeting and nabbing Jude, if possible, at one p.m. We need him. If you can do some research on his latest book so we can have a head start. Once that is finished, you're free to do some sightseeing, then go out for dinner or catch a show, then we fly home Monday at twelve-thirty." He sat up and smiled. He linked his fingers and pushed them out so his fingers clicked. He pushed himself away from the table. "Ladies, you may go. Have a good day being tourists. Any problems, call me." We nodded and collected our bags from the floor. Courtney was still drooling over him.

We said our goodbyes and walked out of his suite.

"Where first?" I asked Courtney as we stood outside Morgan's room. It had just gone midday.

"Fancy hitting the shops? I need an outfit for tonight, plus, we have Morgan's black Amex." She smirked at me.

"Sounds like a plan. Even though I brought a couple of dresses, it wouldn't hurt to look. Let's go shopping." I smiled at her.

We jumped into a taxi outside the hotel. As I got in, I

typed into Google the French words for clothes shops. The taxi driver looked at us and raised his eyebrows. Courtney rummaged around in her bag and pulled out Morgan's black Amex and waved it at him. "Oui, oui." He nodded with a big smile on his face.

"See? He understood that over your silly phone translator." She scowled.

Ten minutes later, we arrived at our destination. We weren't sure where our destination was, but we were there. We were outside a beautiful row of shops; the clothes were amazing. Some of the few shops we saw were the classic designers like Versace, Louis Vuitton, and Yves Saint Laurent. We walked straight into Versace like excited schoolgirls. I felt out of my comfort zone. The dresses in there were way out of my league. Courtney was like a kid in a sweet shop. She darted straight to a leather mini dress, grabbed a size six, and ran off to the changing room. I followed her like a lost puppy, not making eye contact with any of the sales assistants. I sat in the chic dressing rooms on a little stool. I knotted my fingers while I waited for her. I could hear her huffing and puffing and talking to herself. I got my phone out and started scrolling when a message came through.

Hey, can you call me? I need to talk to you, and no, it's nothing to do with Carter X

It was Laura. Wondering what she wanted, I typed a

response telling her I would call her in the .
out on a work dinner later and hoped she wa

I was distracted when I heard the ch.
curtain open to show Courtney in her outfit. .
amazing.

The tight leather bandeau mini fitted he.
perfectly. Her breasts sat perfectly in the dress, giving
slight cleavage. The skirt came up slightly in the middle .
met a few inches up her thigh. She looked amazing.

"Wow, Courtney." I was speechless.

"Does it look okay?" she questioned me, with a
concerned look on her face. This was the first time I had
seen her insecure.

"Courtney, you look stunning. Honestly, your legs look
never-ending. The dress hugs your body so perfectly." I was
in awe. "You need incredible shoes!" I squealed. "What size
are you?"

"A five."

I ran out of the changing room, looking for the perfect
set of heels. After a few minutes of searching, I found a
beautiful black lace up sandal with a four-inch stiletto heel,
and they were a size five. It was meant to be. I ran back into
the changing room and handed her the shoes. Once she
finally laced them up, she smiled at herself in the mirror.

"Courtney, you honestly look amazing. Please buy it.
How much is it?"

She looked at the price tag and swallowed hard. "Freya,

't buy this!"

"Why? How much is it?"

"€2,700! I can't. Morgan will go mad."

"Hey, he wanted us to come on this trip. He told us to
uy ourselves an outfit for tonight. You look amazing and
I'm sure he will agree. Not that I'm saying anything should
happen between you two, but he won't be able to keep his
eyes off you."

She looked down at her shoes and tucked her long
blonde waves behind her ears. She took one more look at
herself in the mirror. "Fine. I suppose I do look hot." She
smirked. There she was; she was back.

After she finally got out of her dress and shoes, we
walked towards the till. She handed the sales assistant the
little leather dress and her sandals. She held Morgan's Amex
anxiously in her hand.

"Okay, ce sera €3800 s'il vous plaît," the assistant said.

Courtney looked at me and shrugged.

"Excuse me, English, please?" I felt awful asking but
my French lessons in school were a distant memory.

"€3,800 euros. Please," she said abruptly. Courtney
handed over the Amex as the cashier snatched it from her
hand and swiped it through the card machine. She smiled
and handed Courtney the Amex back and a Versace bag
which held her beautiful purchases.

"Well, she was a delight, wasn't she?" Courtney said as
we walked out of the shop.

We had popped into a few different shops and I couldn't find anything I liked. "Let's just go home. I've had enough. I'm sure I can find something in my case," I said, defeated.

"No. We will find you a dress. Come on. There are a few shops around the corner."

I sighed. I really didn't want to shop anymore. I was hungry and I needed a drink.

As we walked around the corner. I saw a Louis Vuitton. I clutched my beautiful Louis bag that Carter bought me. My throat went dry.

"Come on. Let's look in here," Courtney said.

I wasn't feeling hopeful. We walked around aimlessly, and just as I was about to give up, I saw a dress hidden behind a pair of high-waisted trousers. It had a lace top with a V-neck plunge. The lace had a nude body vest underneath. There was a sequin band separating the lace from the skirt. The skirt then hung just above the knee. There was one left. A size 10.

"Okay, so I'm going to try this on. Please be truthful."

"Am I anything but truthful?" she said sarcastically. We walked into the changing room. The floor to ceiling mirrors were brightly lit; it was so sophisticated. I went behind the curtain and sighed as I undressed myself. I slipped the dress up my thighs and slid my arms into the lace sleeves. I looked at myself in the mirror. I was surprised it went up my thighs and over my arse. I turned to look at the back of it and noticed a ribbon that tied round the back of the dress.

"Hey, Court? Can you tie me up, please?" I said as I opened the curtain.

"Oh, Freya, wow. You look amazing. That dress!"

"Oh, stop it. I said be truthful, not sarcastic." I rolled my eyes

"I am being truthful. You look beautiful. You little rocket, you!"

I threw her a puzzled look. "Rocket?"

"Yes, a rocket. You know, like, out of this world! Freya, honestly! You just need a pair of sandals with a heel. We will grab them on the way out. Come on. Let's do some more damage."

Luckily for us, this lady spoke English. "That will be €4,200." I threw Courtney a look. *Oh, God. I hope Morgan doesn't lose it.*

CHAPTER TEN

We arrived back at the hotel at four-thirty. I was nervous to give Morgan his card back. We jumped in the lift and went up to our floor. We walked down the hallway and knocked on Morgan's door. My heart was thumping. Courtney decided I should tell him seeing as I was the oldest and my outfit cost more.

"Afternoon, ladies. Did you get everything you needed?" He smiled as he welcomed us into his room.

"I think so." I smiled nervously. Oh my God. I was sweating.

"Show me?" He sat down on the sofa in the lounge area of the suite and muted the television. I nudged Courtney forward so she could show him first.

"Versace. Very nice, Courtney," he said. She took her wrapped dress out of the bag and slowly pulled the wrapping paper off it. She held it up in front of her so he could see. He raised his eyebrows and cleared his throat.

"Wow, what a dress," he choked out.

"Is it too much? Shall I return it?" she mumbled as she started to put the dress back in the bag.

"No. No, not at all. I think it will look lovely. I just wasn't expecting to see so much of you." His eyes burned into her. There was definitely some sexual chemistry there. I was worried before that something would happen on this weekend away, now I was sure that something would.

"Anyway, it's not about cost, so please don't worry. You could have spent £10,000 and I wouldn't have batted an eyelid. My wife spends that on one pillow." He shook his head. "You think I'm joking? I'm being serious. £10,000 on a pillow that I'm not allowed to lay my head on. You couldn't make this shit up." He smirked. "Now, Freya. What did you get? I can't see you in an outfit like the one Courtney has bought." He eyed Courtney and smiled.

"Er, no. No, mine isn't like that," I muttered. Courtney elbowed me as I stepped past her. I bent down and picked my dress out of my bag and held it up.

Morgan smiled. "Very nice, Freya. So you and very sophisticated. I bet you look wonderful in it."

I blushed. I quickly scooped my dress into a ball and put it back in the bag.

"Here is your card. Thank you, Morgan. We are eternally grateful." I handed him his card which he took from me and put back in his wallet.

"You are most welcome. It's the least I can do since I made you come on this trip last minute and there was the risk that Mr Cole might be here." He looked at me and ran his thumb over his bottom lip. I inhaled deeply. *Fuck. Ignore it, Freya.*

"Well, we're very grateful for this opportunity. So, thank you again for the trip and the clothes." I swallowed hard and looked away from him. I picked my bags up and walked towards the door. "You coming, Court? We need to get ready."

"Coming."

I watched her as she walked past Morgan and threw him a look. He knew he had done wrong. He was staring at his feet. I opened the door and took a step out.

"I'm sorry, Freya. I overstepped the mark. Please. Forgive me." Guilt was written across his face.

I turned to face him and smiled, my insides completely falling apart. I turned back and walked out and straight into our room. I dropped my bags to the floor and face-planted on the bed. I really didn't want to go.

Courtney fell down next to me and propped her elbow up so her hand was resting on the side of her head

"Freya, come on." She sighed. "We need to get ready. Ignore Morgan. He does everything for a reaction and that's exactly what you gave him." She shrugged. "You bit."

I turned to face her. "He knows Carter is here. Why would he make that comment?" I put my face back in my pillow.

"He doesn't know he's here. None of us do. But, if he is

here, then he's here. Nothing is going to change. You were going to run into him sooner or later." She pushed herself up so she was now sitting cross-legged, facing me. "We have so much to do before six-thirty. Stop being a bitch and get up. I'm not having you moping around." She grabbed my arm and started pulling me. "Get up!" She was trying to pull me towards her.

"Fine!" I shouted. "Get off me and I'll get up!" I groaned as I moved and sat up, facing her

"Please, Freya. Let's get dressed, have our dinner, and we can come back here. If he is there then we will deal with it. One step at a time." She smiled at me and rubbed her hand up and down my arm. "Come on." She nudged me as she got off the bed. "I packed a bottle of vodka. I'll pour us a shot." She laughed as she ran over to her bag, waving the bottle at me.

I slid off the bed like a stroppy teenager and walked over to Courtney and our vodka shots.

"Here you go, misog. Take that." She shoved the vodka into my hand.

"To tonight! What will be will be." We clinked our glass tumblers and chucked them back like pros. We both winced as the vodka burned our throats.

"Right, missy. Get in the shower. We have an hour and a half and you need a lot of sorting out. Chop chop!"

After the quickest shower of my life, I sat in front of the dressing table. Courtney literally jumped in the shower as I stepped out. We weren't just work friends anymore, we were real friends. She had seen every part of me. I didn't wash my hair as I only did it that morning and Courtney said she would sort it out for me.

I was faffing and getting myself stressed. My make-up wasn't going to plan. I threw my make-up brush down in temper. Courtney emerged from the shower, wrapped in her towel

"Will you calm it, woman? You're annoying me." She picked the brush up and snatched my make-up bag then emptied it all out. "Do you trust me?"

"Do I have a choice?"

"No."

She pulled my hair off my face and started working her magic. Maybe I needed to hire her full time to make me always look amazing. Fifteen minutes later, she told me to look in the mirror. I didn't recognize the woman staring back at me.

I had smoky eyes with a light pink shimmer over my lids. I had a thin line of eyeliner flicked to finish my eyes. I had an amazing glow from the bronzer she had used, topped off with highlighter to emphasize my cheekbones. My lips were a blush pink matte which she completed with a lip liner to make my already full lips fuller. She was amazing.

"Oh my God. Why are you working for me in a publishing house when you could be doing someone's make-up for money? You are a lost cause working for me!"

She shrugged. "I have to start somewhere, don't I?" She poked her tongue out at me. She continued to pamper me. She pulled the top half my curls up and put them into a bun while leaving the bottom half of my auburn curls to fall down my back. She really did work wonders.

"Thank you, Courtney. I owe you big time." I smiled at her

"Then let me have some alone time with Morgan." She winked at me. I threw her a look. "You owe me." She smiled and skipped off into the bathroom to get ready. She was such a diva. I wished I was like that at twenty-three.

I walked over to the bed and touched the ribbon on my dress which was laid out. It was so soft. I ran my fingers across all the different materials, just taking a moment to let everything sink in. I went for a black lacy thong and matching balcony strapless bra. I slipped into my underwear while Courtney was faffing in the mirror. I watched as she pulled her hair up into the perfect messy bun. Why couldn't mine look like that when I did it? All I seemed to resemble was Miss Trunchbull.

"Nice underwear set. Hoping to pull?" she teased.

"Oh, shut up. I don't get to wear nice underwear anymore as I'm single, so I live in Bridgets and old t-shirt bras! So, yes I am wearing a nice underwear set for a change," I said smugly.

I turned away from her as I slid the dress up my thighs and over my hips. I slowly pulled the lace sleeves up over my arms and slipped my arms through the nude vest that sat underneath the thin layer of lace. I took a deep breath as I faced the floor to ceiling mirror.

"Court, hun, can you do me up?"

She walked over to me and did the zip up on the skirt, then pulled the ribbon which was attached to the sequin belt round my back and tied it into a bow. I ran my hands down the skirt to flatten it slightly.

"Look okay?" I asked nervously.

"You look perfect." She smiled sweetly at me.

"Thank you again, Courtney. Now, get your dress on. It's six-fifteen."

She rolled her eyes at me. "Well, if I didn't have to babysit you, I would have been done half an hour ago."

I held my hands up and widened my eyes to signal I was sorry. She just shook her head and shut herself back in the bathroom. I sat on the edge of the bed as I slipped my black open-toed stiletto sandals on. They had a delicate ankle strap which sat in a gold buckle. I put some gold studs in that I picked up from a little accessory stall and grabbed my black clutch out of my suitcase. I threw my cards and phone into the bag along with my matte lipstick. I gave myself a good spray with my Chanel No.5 then gave myself one last look in the mirror.

It will all be okay. Everything will be fine.

I smiled back at myself. Just as I was about to call Courtney, she came out of the bathroom. She looked flawless. Honestly, that girl.

"Ready?" she asked, bright-eyed and bushy-tailed.

"Ready as I'll ever be." I took a deep breath. "You look beautiful." We both smiled at each other and made our way to the main lobby.

Let's get this night over with.

We stepped into the lift and went down to the ground floor; my heart was thumping. I was so nervous. I kept knotting my fingers and playing with my hair.

"Stop fidgeting." Courtney side-eyed me.

"I can't help it. I know we're going to bump into him. I can feel it."

"What you can feel is nerves, now stop it. We're here." The lift pinged as we stopped on the ground floor. As they doors slid open, my eyes darted around the hotel lobby, constantly scanning for him. Courtney took my hand and walked us over to Morgan.

He looked stunning. He was wearing a royal blue suit with tan brogues and a matching belt. He had a white shirt on underneath which, for the first time ever, he'd buttoned all the way up. His hair looked messier, and was brushed to the side. His blue eyes stood out against his black hair and royal blue suit. I had to pick my mouth up off the floor, so I bet Courtney's stomach was doing somersaults.

"Oh, ladies, you look beautiful. Absolutely flawless. I feel extremely lucky having you both on my arm."

"Thank you. You're looking pretty good yourself."

Courtney answered for both of us. He smiled down at her. They actually would make a really nice couple.

He showed us to a waiting car outside. "After you." He placed his hand on the small of my back and ushered me into the car, then did the same to Courtney. I stifled a laugh as I watched her trying to sit ladylike in her mini dress. She glared at me. I pressed my lips into a thin line and looked away from her. The restaurant was only a short car ride away which I was pleased about. Morgan had his head in his phone. Courtney was taking selfies and I was looking out at beautiful Paris.

We pulled up outside the restaurant; my hands felt sweaty. Morgan's driver opened the door for us all to exit. Morgan stepped out first and offered his hand, Courtney got out then re-adjusted her dress, and I stepped out after her. I took a deep breath as we walked up to the restaurant doors. We were greeted by a waiter who quickly ticked us off his list and showed us to our seats. As we were walking over to our table, I looked back at Courtney. We were both looking to see if we could see him; luckily, we couldn't.

The waiter pulled my seat out. I thanked him and took my seat. I laid my napkin over my lap and fidgeted in my seat. We were sitting at a table with a small local publishing house in Paris. Luckily for us, they spoke English. The wine was flowing, the food was amazing, and the entertainment was fantastic. I was trying to pace myself as I didn't want to get drunk in front of Morgan. Courtney was well on her way though. She and Morgan were flirting constantly. I felt like the awkward third wheel. I downed the rest of my wine and excused myself. I slowly stood up and walked to the bathroom. I looked around at everyone enjoying themselves, but I just wanted to go home.

I walked into the bathroom and took a deep breath. My make-up still looked amazing. I applied some more lipstick and washed my hands. I just needed a breather. I closed my eyes for a moment to let my breathing steady. I was disturbed by a young brunette who left one of the cubicles. She was wearing a fitted navy ball gown with a slit up to her thigh. She finished her outfit off with silver strappy sandals. She flicked her long brunette locks over her shoulder and smiled smugly at me. She topped her lipstick up and walked out of the bathroom without saying a word. I looked at myself one last time and walked out of the bathrooms. I noticed the girl from the toilet walking over to her table a few rows behind mine. I stood and watched while grabbing a glass of champagne from a waiter's tray who was walking past. As I studied her, I saw her run her hand across her date's shoulders and take her seat next to him. She turned slightly to face him and smiled. He turned and smiled back at her. I smiled watching them. I stood there in the chaos. As they broke their embrace, he turned to get the waiter's attention. Then, right there, my heart fell out of my chest. Those sage eyes finding mine, my heart started racing. The look on his face must have mirrored mine.

That girl I saw in the toilet was his date.

She had my Carter.

CHAPTER ELEVEN

I stood there, frozen to the spot. I watched as he slowly slid out from his chair and walked over to me. Before I could move, he was there, standing in front of me, his breath on my face, his delicious scent around me. I held my breath and finally looked up at him, our eyes meeting.

"Hello, Freya," he said apprehensively.

"Hey," I replied timidly. I looked past him and saw his date staring at us with a disgusted look on her face.

"Erm, your date is waiting for you." I nodded over to his table.

"Don't worry about her for the minute. She can wait," he said abruptly, looking over his shoulder. She turned away.

"Okay, so I'm going to go back to my table." I looked for Courtney but she was too busy with Morgan. I knotted my fingers.

"No you don't." He smirked. "Follow me outside. I want to talk to you." A smile spread across his face. He brushed past me as he walked towards the lobby area of the restaurant. The electric spark coursed through my body. I gave Courtney one more look, but she was still lost in Morgan. I followed him out, my heart thumping in my chest and ears. I felt sick.

The fresh air hit me as I walked outside. Carter stood slightly in front of me. I could feel his eyes looking me up and down. I walked over to him slowly; nerves were getting the better of me. I could feel my stomach somersaulting. I took a deep breath as I stood in front of him. I was like a moth to a flame. Completely intoxicated in him, and we hadn't even touched. I had to refrain from putting my hands into his hair and pulling him down towards me just so I could kiss him, so I could lose myself in him.

"Freya, as always, you look beautiful," he said in a low, husky voice. I could feel myself blushing.

"You look nice too." I smirked at him. I lied. He looked amazing as usual. He was wearing a navy suit with a white shirt and a navy bowtie. I didn't think I had ever seen him so formal. "What do you want, Carter?"

"Oh, I love it when you're mad." He grinned down at me as he took a step closer.

"I'm not mad. I'm cold." I crossed my arms and looked down at my feet.

"I just wanted to see how you are. We haven't spoken in a year and, well, I didn't know if I would get this opportunity," he replied, running his hand round the back of his head and looking down also. I looked at him as he slowly turned his face up and I saw that grin appear again.

"I'm okay. Being kept busy at work which is good." I nodded. "What about you? You seem happy. I bumped into your girlfriend in the toilet. A bit full of herself but I wouldn't expect anything less. That's what I meant when I said I couldn't be what you wanted. Her, that's not me." I took a breath. Before I could continue, he put his finger over my lip to silence me

"Shh." He wrapped his other arm around me and pulled me in close to him. "For starters, she isn't my girlfriend, she is my date. Secondly, I didn't want you to be like her. I wanted you to be like you." He slowly ran his finger across my lip then started trailing it down my chin and across my jawline. My breath caught. Just feeling his touch against my skin brought everything back. "I've missed you, Freya. More than you could ever know. I had no choice but to let go seeing as Miss Stubborn didn't have the decency to return any of my calls. But, enough about that. Let's not dwell on the past," he whispered.

We stared at each other in silence, not sure what to say. I placed my hands on his chest and bowed my head, closing my eyes. I felt his arms tighten around me, his breathing steadying. We stood still for what felt like hours. We were only pulled from our moment because Carter's phone started ringing. He sighed deeply as he let go of me. I wrapped my arms around myself and stepped back and forth while waiting to see what he was doing. He walked back over, agitated. "That was Chloé."

"Oh, is that your date?"

"Yup." He straightened his bowtie. "Can I see you tomorrow? We're staying in the same hotel."

Shit. It was him last night.

"Oh my God, it *was* you!" I shouted.

"What? When did you see me?"

"Last night, me and Courtney were going into our room and I saw you go into your room with your tongue down someone's throat, which I am now assuming was Chloé," I replied bitterly. "I can't meet you tomorrow. Are you deluded?" I could feel all the emotions coming back. "Carter, do you not understand how much you hurt me? You can't just pick me up, especially now you're with someone new!" My voice was getting louder; passersby were looking. "I shouldn't have come out here with you. What was I thinking?" I shook my head, laughing at myself. "Bye, Carter. Enjoy your trip," I said as I turned away.

I was pulled back round to face him. Before I could say anything, he wrapped his arms around me and lifted me up, his mouth finding mine. His kiss was hungry and fierce. He teased me with his tongue. I opened my mouth with a low moan as we lost ourselves in each other. He placed me down then ran his hands up around my face, slowing his kiss down. He gently planted kisses on my lips. I pulled away and bit my lip.

"Freya, fuck. God, I've missed you," he stammered.

"I've missed you too." I touched my lips. They were on fire. He came towards me and kissed me again, this time softly and more tentatively. I pulled back again. He took my hand and rubbed his fingers across my knuckles.

"You'd better get back to Chloé. She's going to wonder where you are." I took my hand out of his quickly, trying to not let the jealousy get the better of me. "Enjoy your evening. Goodnight, Carter."

I didn't stay to listen to what he had to say. I quickly ran up the restaurant stairs and through the lobby. I passed a waiter with a tray of champagne and took a glass from him, throwing it back. I walked over to my table and saw Courtney's face.

"Where the bloody hell have you been?" She looked frantic. "Seriously, I have been freaking out."

I held my hands up. "I'm sorry. I bumped into Carter." I looked over at his table; he was just sitting back in his seat. He kissed Chloé on the cheek; the same lips that just bought me back to life were now kissing her.

"Oh, Freya. I'm sorry. Did it go okay?"

"It went perfectly. We had the most amazing kiss that set my senses on fire, and five minutes later, he is back sitting playing happy families with her." I felt that familiar lump crawling back up into my throat. *Not here, Freya. Please.*

"It's okay. Don't cry here. Let me say goodnight to

Morgan and we'll leave. We've got a big day tomorrow anyway. I'll meet you in the lobby." She gave me a sympathetic smile. I collected my bag from the table and scurried through the room to get to the lobby. I threw my arm down and let out a deep breath. I needed to cry. I needed to get rid of this lump in my throat. I heard footsteps behind me, and I was grateful Courtney was leaving with me. I turned around to face her, only to see Carter walking towards me.

"Freya, please," he said, sighing. "Meet me tomorrow. I need to see you again."

"I can't do this again, Carter. I can't get hurt again. I'm still not over the last time." I looked at him.

"Freya, I never want to hurt you again. Please, just meet me tomorrow."

Just as I was about to reply, I saw Courtney coming. She pushed past Carter and grabbed my arm.

"Come on, hun. Let's go back to the hotel." We started walking but she turned back to face Carter. "You are not doing this to her again, not on my watch." She scowled.

I looked back at him as he stood there, defeated. We slipped into a waiting cab and headed back to the hotel.

"Thank you, Courtney," I mumbled

"Anytime, sweetie."

I looked out the back of the taxi as it started to pull away and saw Carter standing in the road, watching me drive away. I faced the front and let out a sigh. Before I knew it, tears were streaming down my face.

We finally made it back to the hotel. The traffic was awful as we were driving back. We stepped into the room, I dropped my bag to the floor, then dived into the bed. Courtney went into the bathroom and appeared, fresh-faced and in her pyjamas. Oh, she looked comfy.

"Go and get changed, otherwise you'll have a face full of spots in the morning."

I dragged myself off the bed and went into the bathroom. I cleansed my face then splashed it with cold water. I looked at myself in the mirror. I slowly unpinned my hair and took out my bun. I shook my hair loose. It felt good to have it down. I looked back in the mirror and touched my lips. I flashed back to our kiss. I closed my eyes to savour the moment. I pulled myself back into the room and slowly undid my dress. I let it drop to the floor and stepped out. I walked out into the bedroom and grabbed a clean nightdress from my suitcase and slipped it on. The silk nightdress felt amazing against my skin. I fell back onto the bed next to Courtney who was engrossed in *Dirty Dancing*. I looked beside me and she had put my phone on charge and had poured me a vodka from the mini bar. I looked at my phone and noticed four missed calls from Carter. There was no way I was calling him back. Not tonight, anyway.

I looked over at Courtney who was texting on her phone and smiling like an idiot.

"Who are you talking to?" I questioned, knowing full

well who she was talking to.

"Morgan," she said quickly.

"Courtney, he's married," I said, raising my eyebrows.

"He's actually separated. Has been for a few months." She sighed. "Their divorce is going through once we get home." She smiled weakly.

"Oh, that's sad. They've been married for years." I fidgeted on the bed. Morgan was thirty-four and had been married since he and his wife were twenty-four. I always thought it may have been an arranged marriage as their grandfathers were partners.

"Me and Morgan have been seeing each other for the last few weeks." She spoke nervously. "I didn't want to tell you until we both knew how we felt, but we have fallen hard. I know he is eleven years older than me but I can't not be with him. He sets my soul on fire," she said, smiling at her phone. "We love each other, Freya. You know what I'm talking about because you have it with Carter."

"Had. Had it with Carter," I corrected her. "Do you really love him? I don't want you getting hurt."

"Yes, Freya. I do. Anyway, enough about this. I'm going to see Morgan." She smiled a big smile at me. "Will you be okay?"

I threw a pillow at her. "Of course. I will be fine. I have Patrick Swayze and Jennifer Grey." I beamed at her. "Enjoy your night, but not too much. You're only next door." I smirked at her. "I'll try not to." She winked at me. "Night,

Greene!" she shouted as she shut the door.

I snuggled down into bed and lost myself in *Dirty Dancing*. The nightmare evening was turning into a perfect night in.

I was woken by banging. I rolled over and looked around the room, startled. I didn't know if I had dreamt it or not. I lay back down and got snuggled under the duvet. Just as I closed my eyes, I heard the banging again, which sounded like it was coming from the door. I threw the duvet back and stormed over to the door. "Courtney, why didn't you take your key?" I groaned as I swung open the door.

"Oh," I muttered under my breath. Standing with his hands either side of the doorframe, was Carter.

"Carter, please go. I'm tired. I can't do this tonight," I said, defeated

"No chance," he whispered as a wicked grin spread across his face. He pushed himself off the doorframe, shutting the door behind him. He placed his hands either side of my face. "Freya," he whispered as he kissed me softly. He pulled away and looked deep into my eyes, as if he was looking into my soul. I ached for him. I ran my hands into his tousled hair and pulled him towards me. I kissed him slowly, massaging his tongue with mine. He ran his hands down my body then rested his hands on my hips. Our kiss got fiercer, as if we put all of our emotion into this one moment, this moment that we didn't want to end. He picked me up effortlessly and walked over to the bed, putting me down gently.

"I really have missed you," he mumbled as he rested his forehead on mine.

"I've missed you more," I whispered back to him.

He met my lips and kissed me. His lips were so soft as they were brushing against mine, they felt like the inside of a rose. We both knew where this night was going. I knew it was wrong, but I yearned for him. I needed him. I sat down on the bed and pulled him towards me. I slowly slid back as he kneeled between my legs and made his way to me. He gently tugged on my silk nighty and pulled it down slightly.

"I need to get this off you," he growled.

My stomach was fluttering; a deep pulling and burning sensation down low was taking over my body. I wanted to ask where Chloé was. Had he broken up with her? Did he want me back? Those questions were spinning around my head, but I didn't want to listen. I wanted him. I didn't want anything to stop this from happening.

CHAPTER TWELVE

He slowly came face to face with me, smiling, keeping his eyes on mine the whole time. He slid his hand up my thigh, slowly pushing my silky nightdress up with it. I caught my breath; his touch on my skin was driving me mad. He slowly brushed his fingertips over my black lace thong, awakening my senses. I moaned as he delicately caressed my sweet spot; his soft movements and the lace of my thong were too much. I slowly pushed his hand away. He smirked and lowered himself over me, kissing me softly. He trailed kisses down my jawline, slowly moving down to my neck then onto my collarbone. My breath caught. He pulled at my nightdress and gently untucked my breasts from the delicate silk and lace. He pulled himself away from me, keeping his eyes on mine the whole time. He brought his hand up and cupped my left breast then took it into his mouth, gently sucking and licking my nipple. Once they were hard, he gently blew on them, the sensation of the warmth of his mouth and the cold of his breath was getting too much. He carried on this routine for a few minutes. He slowly slid his free hand down my body against my nightdress and found my underwear. He pulled them to the side, exposing me, his fingers slowly teasing as they brushed against my sweet spot again. He matched the rhythm of his fingers with his tongue on my nipples, slowly moving from one to the other. I started to moan; the different sensations were too much.

"Carter," I moaned. "Please."

"Shh. I'm not ready to stop yet." He grinned up at me. His fingers slowly found me. He slid them slowly, deeply into me. I moaned out loud and arched my back. The whole time he was keeping up this tantalizing rhythm with his mouth and tongue. With each thrust of his fingers, his thumb brushed along my sensitive spot, sending a sweet sensation rippling through my body. I couldn't hold it off anymore; I was climbing and I couldn't slow it. I looked down at him and watched what he was doing; the low street light coming through the hotel window was just enough. Before I could tell him, my body hit its peak. I came hard, crashing around his teasing fingers. He slowly pulled his fingers out and sucked on them.

"Just like I remember. So sweet." I turned crimson as I threw my arm over my face. "Don't be shy. We're only just getting started. We have a lot of making up to do." He grinned down at me. He looked so hot. I sat up and slowly reached up to his chest. I started undoing his buttons. As my hands reached his trousers, I undid his bottoms, slowly sliding them down. I ran my hands up his toned belly, savouring every touch. I slowly pushed his shirt off his shoulders and watched it drop to the floor. He stood up and kicked his trousers off. I perched myself up on my elbows and admired the view.

He grabbed the tops of my thighs and pushed them apart. He lowered himself in between my legs as his mouth covered my sweet spot, his tongue flicking and teasing me. He moved his hands round to my hips as he tightened his grip. He slowly caressed me, my pelvis moving with him. He slowly kneeled up to kiss me. He grabbed the bottom of my night dress and slowly pulled it over my head. I was now sitting in just my thong, him in his boxers. I could see his arousal through his white Calvin Klein's. I pushed him back onto the bed so he was lying down. I climbed on top of him, legs either side. I could feel him underneath me, growing again. He put his hands around my waist and pulled me down towards him, our mouths finding each other. I moaned as his tongue teased mine, our kiss getting deeper. My hands were back in his hair, gently tugging and pulling. He slowly pushed me up so I was off him. I stayed there while he slid his boxers down his legs. He then pulled my thong down. I flicked them off my ankle. I slowly lowered myself back down onto him. I gasped as he filled me, the familiar sting as I took him completely. I started to move slowly on top of him, moaning slightly as he mirrored my movements. He put his hand round the back of my head and gently pulled me down as our mouths met again, our tongues entwining. I thrust my hips back and forward. His breathing started getting heavier; the sensation was overwhelming. I pulled away and looked down at him. It was such a turn on, watching him underneath me, crumbling with every movement. His hands were back on my hips as he moved with me. Each move, he was hitting my sweet spot again and again. I could feel myself building and climbing again.

"Come for me, Freya," he moaned. "You are such a turn on." He groaned as he thrust his hips up against me. I started to speed up slightly as I watched him start his climb.

"Shit, Freya," he said through gritted teeth.

There I was again, the sweet release about to leave my body. It consumed me. I threw my head back as I continued to move with him, my hair falling down my back. Carter tightened his grip on my hips. I couldn't hold it anymore. I let out a moan as I let myself go around him, consuming him as well as myself, the sweet sensation taking over my body once more. He followed me, letting himself go as he moaned my name as he finished.

"Freya, what do you do to me?" He sat up and cradled me, wrapping his arms tightly around me and kissing me, our bodies hot and sweaty, completely lost in each other.

We lay next to each other in silence; no words were needed. The raw emotions hit me; lust, love, and heartbreak. They consumed me. I rolled over and pulled the duvet up to my chest and clutched it tightly, closing my eyes. I felt Carter's weight shift as he wrapped his arms around me. He nuzzled his face into my neck and let out a deep sigh. A few moments passed when I felt Carter press his soft lips against my neck. He trailed them slowly up my jawline. I moved slowly to face him as I found his lips. I just wanted to lose myself again and again in him. I knew it was wrong. Chloé was sleeping in their hotel room, and there we were, naked, wrapped in sheets, kissing after making love.

"I've missed lying with you," he whispered before kissing my earlobe.

"I've missed you too," I whispered. I found his hand and squeezed it. "We are so wrong for doing this." I rolled over to face him so I was lying on my side. "I'm just as bad as Jake and Amy." I scowled and bowed my head.

He put his hand under my chin and lifted it up to look at him. "You are nothing like them," he whispered.

I stared at him, focusing on every little detail. He placed his right hand on the side of my face and slowly rubbed my cheek with his thumb. As much as I wanted to lie there all night, I knew we couldn't. He had to go back to his room.

"You'd better go." I rolled onto my back. "It's early hours and Chloé will wonder where you are. Plus, I have a big day tomorrow and I really do need to sleep."

He placed his hand on my belly. "But I don't want to

go," he said, furrowing his brow

"I don't want you to go, but you're not mine to keep." I smiled weakly at him

"I've always been yours."

"Let's not get into this now. As it stands now, you're with Chloé. You brought her here with you."

"Don't go to see Jude tomorrow. Stay in bed with me," he said, with a smouldering look on his face.

I nudged him with my elbow. "I have to go. It's the whole reason Morgan brought me here. Same reason you're here. To nab Jude from us." I sat up with the bed sheet still wrapped around me. Even though Carter had seen me naked, this felt different. I felt like he was a stranger.

"I didn't come here for Jude," he said bluntly. "I came here for you."

I turned to face him. "Why are you lying? If you came for me, you wouldn't have come with her. Don't bullshit me, Carter." I shook my head as I stood and walked round to the end of the bed.

"Please, Freya. I'm not bullshitting you." He sat up in bed and sighed, his sage eyes burning into mine.

"Well, I am here, but it doesn't change anything. You're with her. Can you just go, please?"

I didn't want him to go. I wanted to stay snuggling into him all night, but I couldn't be that girl.

"Fine. If that's what you want. I'm not going to Jude's signing tomorrow. I will be in my room. Chloé is going home tomorrow morning. The offer is still there to spend the day with me."

He slid off the bed with the bed sheet wrapped around himself. He bent down to pick up his boxers and trousers. He dropped the sheet, revealing his toned bum. He looked over his shoulder and caught me looking. He winked at me while grinning as he pulled his trousers up. He put his shirt on but left the buttons undone. He walked over to me and kissed me delicately. "I don't want to lose you again, Freya."

I smiled and looked down at my feet. Carter didn't move from in front of me. I swallowed hard and looked back up at him. "How can you lose something you never had?"

He slowly tucked a strand of my auburn hair behind my ear and kissed me once more. "You know where I will be tomorrow. Just me and you. Think about it." He looked over his shoulder at me one last time before opening the door and leaving. I finally stopped holding my breath.

Shit.

I snuck back into bed. It was three a.m. All of a sudden, I felt exhausted. My skin was still tingling. How could he have this effect on me? I rolled over on my side and tucked the corner of the duvet under my cheek and started to doze.

I woke disorientated. I had slept so heavily. I rolled over and checked my phone. Eleven a.m. I sighed. We were meant to be meeting Jude in a couple of hours. Courtney hadn't even been back to the room. I went to the bathroom to freshen up; my body ached from last night's events. I stepped into the shower and stood under the hot water for a few moments. I washed my hair and smothered the ends in conditioner. It felt so dry. I closed my eyes as I slowly lathered soap all over my body, re-tracing the lines Carter had traced, my skin reacting to my touch. I slowly ran the soap over my still sensitive breasts then moved down to my delicate spot. I gasped as the sensation hit my body once more. I ached for him again. I opened my eyes and came back to reality. I rinsed my hair off and stepped out of the shower. I walked through to our room and picked my phone up. I opened my messages and started typing one to Courtney;

Hey, it's me. I have been up all night being sick, not sure if it's something Ive eaten or a bug. Please apologize to Morgan for me xx

I sat on the hotel bed with my hair dripping wet. I found Laura on my call list and clicked call.

"Hello?"

"Hey, it's me. Sorry I haven't called before. Been a bit manic since I've been here."

"Hey! Don't be silly. How is it there? Have you seen Carter yet?"

Balls. I can't lie to her. She knows when I'm lying, even though I'm on the other end of the phone.

"Erm, yeah. I have."

"Oh, hun. Are you okay? That must have been awful."

"Yeah, it wasn't great." I sighed. "At first, anyway."

"Oh, Freya... you didn't..." I could hear the disgust in her voice already.

"Yeah, I did. We both got so caught up in the moment, emotions got in the way, and well, you know, one thing led to another..."

"Oh dear God. Freya, how could you be so stupid to get yourself in that position with him again?" she asked, raising her voice.

"Okay, Lau. Enough, please. I'm big enough and ugly enough to know what I'm doing. Anyway, don't worry. There's nothing to worry about."

"I don't believe you."

"Well, do. Anyway, you needed to tell me something?"

"Yeah, I do. I just feel it's not the right moment now."

"Don't be ridiculous, Lau. Tell me!" I said, agitated.

"Fine! Fine, well, erm, me and Tyler are expecting!"

"OMG! I am so happy for you!" I screeched.

"Thank you, darling!"

"How far gone are you? Oh, I'm so excited."

"I'm sixteen weeks. We're having a little girl."

I started jumping up and down on the spot. "Yes! A little girl to join our group. Oh, Lau, I want to squeeze you. Well, not too hard, obviously, but argh! Congratulations to you and Tyler. I can't wait to see you when I'm back!"

"Hurry back. I can't wait to see you either." I could hear the smile in her voice. "Anyway, I've got to go. I will see you when you're home, sweetie. Please be careful. Love you."

"I will. Love you too."

As soon as the phone was cut off, I started jumping up and down on the spot, screaming again, when I was interrupted by someone coughing.

"Sickness bug, eh?" Courtney said, sounding pissed off.

"I can explain," I stammered.

"Please do," she said, standing there with her arms crossed, her brows furrowed.

I rolled my eyes at her. Who did she think she was? She spent the night with Morgan in his hotel suite and now she was acting like my boss.

"Don't be like this, Court. I spent the night with Carter," I said nervously.

"Did you?" she replied, surprised.

"I did. This is our last day. I need to see what this is. I need to know if this is real or whether it was just mixed emotions that got us into this mess. This is my last chance. You can understand that, surely?"

She dropped the act and walked over to me. "Of course I understand. Just don't lie to me." She wrapped her arms around me and hugged me tight. "I can take care of Jude with Morgan. Just keep your head down. You don't want to piss Morgan off." She let go of me. "Anyway, I've only come to get a change of clothes then I'm heading back next door. We'll talk properly tonight. I want to know every detail, missy." She beamed. She ran around the room, grabbing her things. She blew me a kiss as she ran back out the door.

"Young love," I muttered under my breath as I walked over to my suitcase.

CHAPTER THIRTEEN

I rummaged through my suitcase for something to wear. Seemed a bit pointless, as, no doubt, my clothes would be off for most of the day. I blushed at the thought. I settled on a white t-shirt and my skinny jeans. I pulled my hair up into a high ponytail and pulled a couple of loose bits out, which sat round my ears. I sat down on the bed and checked my phone. Nothing from Carter. I started panicking that I wasn't going to see him. Maybe he didn't want to see me. Maybe my bratty behaviour last night had put him off. I didn't actually agree to seeing him. I unlocked my phone and opened a message:

Hey you, still around today? F x

I sat, anxiously waiting for his response. A few minutes later, my phone beeped. It was him.

Of course. Come now. Room 406 x

I sprayed some of my Chanel No.5 and touched my face up with a bit of bronzer and lip gloss. I was excited and nervous at the same time. I grabbed my room key and put that and my phone in my back pocket. I looked down the hallway as I left my room, just in case Morgan was out there at the same time as me. I quickly ran over to Carter's room; I still couldn't believe I saw him the other night. I shuddered at the thought of him kissing and being with someone other than me. It was a bitter pill to swallow. I stood outside his hotel room and took a deep breath before knocking. I looked down at my feet while I waited, and the door slowly opened. I looked up and gasped. It wasn't Carter staring back to me, it was Chloé.

"Hello, homewrecker," she snarled at me.

"Excuse me?" I answered, shocked. "I'm not a homewrecker."

"Are you not? Did you spend the night with my boyfriend last night?" she asked, raising her eyebrows.

"He told me you were his date," I answered quietly.

She laughed as she took a step closer. "Seems like Carter can't tell the truth," she said, smirking. "Stay the fuck away from my man. You are nothing but a desperate whore."

I had to resist reacting, to not stoop to her level.

"Fuck off, Chloé," I said, lashing out at her.

I turned on my heel. I wasn't getting into this with her. I just wanted to get back to my room. I jumped as I heard her scream out at me. I turned to face her, but as I did, she was in my face. She pushed me to the floor and straddled me, pinning my arms down with her knees. She used one hand to grab and pull my hair, and the other to continuously slap my face and head. I used all my strength to push my arms up so I could get her off me. I freed my arms and shoved her back with force. She fell backwards and hit her head on the hotel floor. I got on my knees and steadied my breath. Just as I was about to get up, she got a second wind and launched herself back, throwing her arms around. I felt a sting to the side of my eye, and I threw my arms up to my face to try and shield myself.

"Get off me, you psycho!" I screamed at her. Just as I was going to throw a fist at her, I heard his voice.

"Chloé!" he shouted. "Get the fuck off her!" He ran up behind her, wrapped his arms around her, and dragged her off. She was screaming and clawing at Carter's hands.

"Get off me! She's a fucking homewrecker and a whore!" She started spitting as Carter dragged her into the room, slamming the door behind him.

I crawled up against the wall and threw my head in my hands, trying to calm my breathing. I winced as my fingers caught the side of my eye. I looked at my fingers and noticed blood. I panicked, pulled my phone out, and opened the front camera.

"Shit. That bitch," I muttered. She had obviously caught me with her ring. I tilted my head back and rested it on the wall. The tears started to flow. I heard the hotel room door open, and I quickly dabbed my eyes. Carter frogmarched Chloé down the end of the hallway and put her in the lift. I watched as she tried to plead with him, but he wasn't having any of it. He dropped his head, held his hand up, and turned his back on her. I stared at her. She kept her eyes on mine until the doors shut. I had a feeling this wasn't over.

Carter joined me on the floor and sighed. "Geez, Freya. Your eye." He gently brushed his thumb across it. "We should sort that out. Come." He started to get up, but I grabbed his hand and pulled him back down. "Please, just sit with me." I half-smiled at him.

"Baby, I'm so sorry. I left the room to speak to reception. She told me she would be gone by the time I got back."

I nodded. "I text you as I hadn't heard from you. I thought you'd changed your mind," I mumbled. I unbent my legs and kicked my Converse together, puckering my lips.

"Never, Freya. I told you. I don't want to lose you again."

I just sat there.

"Honestly, Freya. I don't. This past year has been hell." He sighed. "Yes, Chloé was more than a date, but I made it very obvious that it was just a 'thing'." He looked at me, searching for my response. I just stared in front of me. "Chloé knew this was going to happen, especially knowing what would happen if I saw you again. She was my therapy, in a way, after everything. I didn't want to tell my mum and

Ava as I didn't want them to hate me. They love you so much." I looked up at him. *They love me?* Just as I went to speak, he carried on. "But not as much as I do." His eyes widened, and he looked lost. He was staring deep into my eyes. He moved closer to me, steadying his breath. "I really do," he whispered, his lips brushing against mine. I just wanted to climb onto his lap there and then and devour him in the hotel hallway

"Come on. Let's continue with our day. But before the fun starts, let's sort your eye out."

I smiled, and he gave me his hand and helped me up

"She was a crazy bitch," I mumbled as he walked me into his room.

Carter's room was the same as Morgan's. He slumped down on the bed and eyed me up and down. He looked exhausted and it was only midday.

"What a morning, eh?" I walked over seductively to Carter. I wrapped my arms around his neck and stood in between his legs. I leaned down and kissed him gently. I played with the hair on the nape of his neck. His hands wrapped around my waist as our kiss got more passionate. He pulled away. "Can we just talk? As much as I want to take my rage out on you," he said flirtatiously.

My insides were screaming. I needed him. The dull, agonizing ache that needed to be released was taking over. "Talk?" I didn't want to talk.

"Because, we've never done this. We've never spent the

day together just talking. I don't want this relationship to be based solely on sex. We have a better connection than that. Don't get me wrong, the sex is out of this world." He grinned up at me, biting his lip. He lay on the bed and propped himself up then patted the bed next to him. "Come," he said with a cheery smile on his face.

I rolled my eyes, crawled up the bed, and sat down next to him.

It was so nice seeing him in casual clothes. Don't get me wrong, he looked so goddamn hot in a suit, but there was something about seeing him in casual clothes that made me want him more. He was wearing a tight-fitted white t-shirt which showed off his toned, muscular arms, and grey cuffed jogging bottoms which didn't leave much to the imagination when it came to his groin area.

"Oh, baby, don't sulk." He picked up my hand and kissed it. "I promise I will satisfy your every need later. We've got the whole day together," he said smoothly. I glared at him and pouted.

"So, what do you want to talk about, Mr Cole?" I said sarcastically, emphasizing his name. I rolled on my side and rested my hand on the side of my face, my elbow sinking into the duck-feather pillows.

He sighed at me. "I don't know off the top of my head. I just wanted to chill with you." He laughed. I raised my eyebrows at him. "Stop pressuring me!" He raised his voice before breaking into another laugh. I laughed with him.

It was four p.m., and we had lay chatting most of the afternoon, stealing a little kiss here and there.

"As much as lying here doing nothing and chatting has been lovely, we actually do need to have a serious talk." he said quietly. I nodded in agreement. I went to speak and he shook his head. "No, my darling. It's my turn to talk." I widened my eyes then threw him a smirk.

He sat up and crossed his legs, sitting opposite me. He put his hands on my thighs and gave them a little squeeze. I placed my hands on his. They looked so small against his giant hands.

"I need you back in my life. Not like this. Not like before." He choked on the words. "I can't lose you again." He looked scared, and I just wanted to scoop him up and tell him I wasn't going anywhere, but I wanted to see what else he had to say. I didn't say anything, just rubbed my thumb over the back of his knuckles.

"I kicked myself as soon as I left you in Elsworth, in that prick's arms," he said with rage in his voice. He took a deep breath and calmed himself. "I love you more than you will ever know. I know this is one of the first times I'm telling you this, but I do. I fucking love you. I don't want to be with anyone else. I want to marry you, have babies with you, and do all the grown up stuff." He looked at me, searching my face for something.

"Wow. Okay, I wasn't expecting that," I said, still trying to take in everything he had just said. "Can you just give me a few moments to process this? It's a lot to take in." I slid off the bed and walked around the room. *Oh my God. Where the hell has this come from?*

I took some deep, slow breaths as I looked out the hotel window over beautiful Paris. I stood still, watching the rush beneath me. I looked down to see Carter's arms wrap around me. He spun me round to face him. "Please, don't freak out. This has been eating me up since I left you. The amount of times I wanted to call and tell you but you wouldn't answer. I knew you were going to be here. Laura told me. I told her not to tell you because I knew you wouldn't have come and I needed to see you. I know you feel the same. Please tell me you feel the same?"

My eyebrows furrowed, my mouth slightly open, trying to take it all in. *Laura told him I was going to be here, that cow. This was all planned? Were Morgan and Courtney in on this as well?* The questions were flying around my head while trying to deal with everything Carter had just offloaded to me. I closed my eyes for a few minutes, trying to gather my thoughts. I took a big breath and started to speak. "I love you too. I've loved you since our first date. You've broken my heart over and over again. I honestly don't think it could take anymore, Carter. You are my person. My person I want to spend my life with, but I need this to slow down. It's been a day. One whole day and we're back here again. Carter, this can't fuck up again. This needs to be for real. No more of these 'flavours of the month'. I told you once, I'm not that girl. If you want me and only me, and I want you and only you, then we will be fine. We're destined to be with each other. I feel like I've just been walking this Earth searching for you without realizing. My soul needs you, and so does my body." My lips parted slightly as my breath caught. I dropped the hint, hoping he would realize, and lucky for me, he did.

"I promise you, you and me, just us two. I have only felt alive since meeting you. Freya, I love you." His eyes glazed over. He came towards me and found my mouth, his tongue exploring, caressing my tongue on every stroke. I moaned as my body slowly released itself into him. His hands were in my hair, tugging gently. He pulled my head back and started kissing my neck, stealing a few nips here and there. I ran my hands down his t-shirt and placed my hands under it, feeling his toned body. I then slowly traced my finger across the top of his jogging bottoms, smirking as he watched me. I dropped down on my knees and pulled his trousers down, freeing his manhood; he was so hard. I slowly started teasing him, flicking the end of his penis with my tongue. He took a deep breath as I took him into my mouth, then I slowly pulled him out and ran my tongue up and down his shaft. As I flicked the top of his penis again, he took another deep breath.

"Stop. I don't want to come like this. Plus, we're in front of the window," he said, looking down at me with a wicked grin on his face.

I stood up and put both hands on his chest, and tiptoed so my mouth was next to his ear. "Don't be such a wimp," I whispered.

A smile spread across his face. "A wimp? Oh, you wait," he teased.

CHAPTER FOURTEEN

The windows in the hotel were floor to ceiling; they let so much light into the room and the views were just breathtaking.

"Take your clothes off," Carter demanded. "Just leave your knickers on." He smirked. He was still standing there with just his t-shirt on.

"Take your clothes off," I replied. Before I had even taken off my socks, he was completely naked. My belly flipped, and my mouth went dry. He was so hot; his tanned, sun-kissed skin, his sage green eyes hungry for me. He was a God.

"Your turn, Miss Greene," he said as he walked closer to me. "Off. Now."

I slowly took my t-shirt off and threw it on the floor. I undid my jeans and slid them down my legs, kicking them off. I bent down to take my socks off then undid my bra and held it in my hand.

"You're looking good, Freya," he teased. He bit his lip

as I dropped my bra to the floor. There Carter was standing like a God, still hard. Then there was me, standing in my white lace thong, feeling nervous and insecure, like it was our first time.

"My, oh my. What a sight," he said in a low voice. He ran his finger from my shoulder slowly down to my sweet spot. He ran his finger over my lace thong a few times, caressing me in the right place. I let out a moan. He silenced me by putting his hand over my mouth.

"Shh. Don't make a sound," he whispered. He turned me around in front of the window so I was facing the city. He stood behind me as he placed my hands either side of the window. I could feel his penis hard on my bum cheeks. His fingers teased me as he ran his fingertips underneath my bum and along my creases. He then ran them down my thighs and into the middle. He gently pushed in a gesture for me to open my legs. I did what he wanted. He went back to caressing my bum where he traced his finger from cheek to cheek. After a few moments, he stopped and moved his hand underneath me. He cupped my sex then slowly caressed the inside of me with his middle finger. It was such a turn on. Looking out over busy Paris while my hot God pleasured me. He didn't remove my thong, but pushed the material inside me with his finger. The lace and his fingers against me felt amazing. I moaned as he continued. He pulled his finger out slowly and pulled my thong to the side.

"Oh, I'm one lucky bastard," he muttered as he

caressed my bum. He slowly moved to his knees then started planting sweet, gentle kisses over each of my cheeks, nipping occasionally. Every time he nipped, I threw my head back and I felt my auburn hair fall down my back. He ran his hand between my legs again and pushed them further apart. He then put his hands on my hips and pulled my hips and legs back slightly so my top half was positioned more forward. He moved back down and started to explore my sex with his tongue. He started off slowly, as if he wanted to savour every moment. I closed my eyes as the ripples ran through my body, his tongue hitting all the right places. He got deeper the more I moaned; I didn't want him to stop. He then slid two fingers into me while holding my hip with his free hand. He didn't change the momentum; it was deliciously sweet. While his fingers were working their magic, he was kissing my bum again, still nipping when I moaned. My moans were getting louder.

"Stop," I moaned, but he didn't; he continued to devour me. "Carter, please!"

Again, he didn't stop. I could feel myself beginning to climb. I didn't want to come like this. I wanted him. I needed him. Just as I was about to call him again, he stopped. I took a deep breath and steadied myself. I felt him standing behind me. He kissed my earlobe then whispered, "I'm going to fuck you now."

He sent a shiver through me. I was hungry for him. I hadn't realised, but I was panting. He put one hand on my hip and used the other to put himself inside me. As he slowly entered me, his other hand found its way back on my hip as he started thrusting hard into me. I moved my hips back and forth so I was moving with him, and he let out a low groan. He then began to move faster and deeper, crashing into me. I moaned as he hit into me again and again. The build-up was climbing, that delicious ache and burn deep, deep down was beginning to surface. I started to claw my fingers into the wall. I felt like I was going to explode. He gave my hips a gentle squeeze as he moaned. I could tell he was getting close. He grabbed my ponytail with one hand and pulled my head back as he hit me deeper and harder. I felt myself ready to crumble. "I'm going to come," I moaned out as Carter carried on. I orgasmed hard and shattered around him. Carter groaned as he came, crashing down from his high.

We were lying in bed, both still naked. I snuggled under Carter's arm, neither of us saying a word, just taking everything in.

"I'm hungry. Can we get room service?" I asked him, still refusing to move from the same spot I had been lying in for nearly half an hour.

"Why don't we go into the hotel restaurant to eat? It is your last night."

"I don't want to get dressed, and to be honest, I don't want to run into Morgan and Courtney." I shuffled and nuzzled into him more. "Plus, this is sooo much better than sitting in a restaurant."

He tutted at my comment. "Fine. Let's order room service, but, as soon as we're home, I'm taking you out." He picked up the phone and began ordering for me.

Once he put the phone down, I let out a sigh. What was to say we would be like this once we got home, back to work and normal life? Everything always feels better when you're on holiday. I sat up in bed, now conscious that I was naked in front of him. I shuffled forward slightly. Carter followed and sat up against the headboard.

"What's wrong?" he asked.

"I'm worried."

"Why are you worried?" His brow furrowed.

"What if this is just the honeymoon period? We couldn't make it work before, so what's to say it will work this time?"

"Freya." He shuffled next to me and scooped me into his embrace. "I told you, I won't lose you again. This is it. You're stuck with me. I will make you my wife," he said sternly.

I felt butterflies in my stomach. His wife. I would be Mrs Cole. I know it was wrong of me, but I just didn't believe him. He promised me so much before and that all ended as quickly as it started. I was a doubter, unfortunately, and I became even worse after Jake cheated on me.

He kissed my neck, whispering, "I promised you, Freya. It's just me and you."

I wriggled away from him. I wanted to believe him but he would have to prove it.

I slipped out of bed and into the bathroom, locking the door behind me. I sat on the closed toilet and took a minute. I opened up my phone and had a scroll through Instagram. *I wonder if Carter has Instagram.* I shook the thought away while casually double tapping on the photos of people I didn't know. I was distracted when I heard a knock on the bathroom door.

"Everything okay, baby?" Carter asked.

"Yeah, fine. Just needed the loo." I blushed as I responded.

"No problem," he muttered as he walked away from the door.

Why am I being such a bitch? He's told me he can see us getting married, having children, and I've locked myself in his bathroom, sitting on the toilet, scrolling through bloody Instagram. I needed to sort myself out. I came out of Instagram and closed the app. I needed to get off it and back out to Carter. I slowly stood from the toilet and walked over to the sink while looking in the mirror. There it was. My glow. I smiled at my reflection. I threw the hotel bathrobe around me. I grabbed my phone off the sink unit and unlocked the door. Carter was standing outside, waiting for me.

"You sure you're okay?"

"I'm fine. It's just... this afternoon has been a bit of a

whirlwind." I smiled at him. "I've gone from coming here, worried I was going to see you, to then seeing you. We then slept together and you poured your heart out to me. It's not even been twenty-four hours. I just feel overwhelmed. My brain can't register what's happened." My panicked eyes searched his the whole time.

"Baby, I'm sorry. I didn't mean for you to feel like that. I just needed to tell you everything." He rested his forehead against mine. "You've changed me. I've never felt like this before and I'm absolutely terrified I will lose you again." Our eyes burned into each other's. "I won't lose you again," he whispered.

He looked so vulnerable. It was weird seeing him that way. He looked like a lost boy who needed to be guided home.

I wrapped my arms around his waist and snuggled into his chest, his heart slowing down. I felt his shoulders relax.

"Let's just take one day at a time, yeah?" I suggested. Like I'd said, it had been a crazy twenty-four hours.

We were interrupted by a knock.

"That must be dinner." He gently pulled my arms from his waist and walked towards the door, greeting the server. "Good evening," he said politely as he took the plates off and quietly closed the door behind him. "Hungry?"

"Famished," I said, my belly growling.

I sat on the bed as Carter handed me my plate; steak and chips with peppercorn sauce. One of my favourites. I smiled. I love my food.

I put the first bit in my mouth; it melted as soon as it hit my tongue.

We both sat in silence as we enjoyed our food. The dinner reminded me of when Carter cooked for me. It was our second date, and he took me to Birchwood, his stunning London house. It also reminded me of the conversation we had when he asked me to be one of his ladies. I pushed that memory out of my head as quickly as I could. Maybe that was why he had ordered this for me; to remind me of one of our early dates. I pushed my plate away. I had eaten it so fast I had given myself indigestion. I walked away and picked up a bottle of water from the side and took a big few mouthfuls.

"You okay, babe?" he asked.

"Fine. Just ate too fast." I rolled my eyes at myself. Such a greedy bitch.

"Glad you enjoyed it." He smiled at me.

"I should really go. Need to catch up with Courtney. No doubt I have loads of work to do." I put the bottle back down on the side.

"Don't go. Stay the night. You leave tomorrow," he said, pulling a sad face then winking at me when he saw me thinking about it.

"Oh, I don't know. I should really get back." I pulled my phone out of my back pocket and gave it a quick glance. Nothing. I looked back up when I saw him walking towards me seductively.

"You really shouldn't." He grinned. Before I could argue back, he kissed me, pushing me back on the desk where I had just put my water down. I wanted to pull away. I wanted to go back to my room just so I could take everything in, but I couldn't. I couldn't pull away from him. He ran his hand down and pushed my legs apart, moving in between them. He put his hands up to my face and cradled it. My heart beat faster as his kiss became deeper. I knew where this was leading; my tummy was in knots. The familiar burning was back and it needed putting out. He lifted me gently onto the desk, pushing me back slightly. I gasped as I saw the want in his eyes. He needed me like I needed him. His lips kissed my neck and he slowly moved his way down to my collarbone, his hands fumbling around the tie on my dressing gown. He slowly pulled it and pushed the gown away. The gown was falling off of my shoulder. I wanted to take it off, but Carter wouldn't let me. He seemed to like the fact that I was completely naked under there. His hands slowly smoothed over my skin, past my hips and down to my thighs. His fingers found my sweet spot, slowly entering me, teasing me on every thrust. He loved the fact that I was ready for him. I bit my lip as I watched him. He broke his kisses from my body. He ran his finger along my jaw and slowly tilted my chin back, smiling at me. He covered my mouth with his. We were so hungry for that moment. His tongue continued invading my mouth. He pulled away and smiled down at me as he carried on with this delicious rhythm. He moved down to my breasts, flicking his tongue across my nipple before taking it into his mouth. I was building once again. I didn't want it to end. I could feel his smile on my skin. He relished the fact that my body responded to his every touch. I moaned as he put me under his spell, his kisses smothering every exposed part of my body as he lost himself in me. I was his; this time it felt real and I loved it.

CHAPTER FIFTEEN

I woke up hot. I looked over my shoulder to see Carter wrapped around me. It was lovely but I was so used to my own space in bed, I felt smothered. I slowly moved his arms then sat up and gently lifted his leg off mine. He muttered something in his sleep as he rolled completely over. I felt so rested; I slept so much better when I knew where he was. I stepped out of bed, made a call on the hotel phone to reception, and ordered a big pot of tea and two cups. I smiled as I put the phone down. It was seven-thirty a.m. I looked down at my attire; Carter's t-shirt. I put it up to my nose and smelled. I smiled. My flight to London was leaving at twelve-thirty; I really needed to go back and pack. I walked round to his side of the bed and just watched him. His mousy brown tousled hair was even messier than usual after last night. His faint freckles over his nose and cheeks were barely there now. His lips were puckered and slightly open, his breathing calm. He looked so relaxed. I felt incredibly lucky to have him back in my life.

I was torn away from my beautiful sight when I heard a knock on the door. I quickly tiptoed over and quietly opened the door. I thanked the waiter and took the tray from him. I shut the door with my foot and placed the tray on the desk. The same desk where me and Carter had sex last night. I blushed. It was so hot. Normally, our sex was pretty vanilla, but that time felt different. There was more want and need. We were so hungry for each other, nothing stopped us from letting out our inner freaks.

I rubbed my lips together to distract me. I started making our tea when I heard Carter stirring. I looked over my shoulder and smirked. "Good morning, handsome." I walked over to him with his cup of tea and planted a gentle kiss on his lips. He took the cup of tea from me and sat up.

"Good morning, beautiful." His mouth broke into his beautiful smile as he took a sip of tea. "Mmm, that is a good cup of tea. I could get used to this." He winked at me.

I picked up my own cup and joined him in bed. As I sat down, he kissed my forehead. My tummy somersaulted.

"So, what's going to happen when we're back home?" I asked. "I leave in a few hours, then it's back to life."

He reached over and put his cup on the bedside table then faced me. "I think we should live together," he said, all chipper.

"Do you not think it's a bit soon?" I questioned, panicking. "I only said last night that I want to take things one step at a time and you're saying about us living together.

I just meant with us. What are we going to do?"

He took my hand. "Please calm down." He shook his head, smiling at me. "I'm not saying that we should move in together right away, but I do want to live with you."

I bit my lip. I didn't know what to say. I knew deep down that I wanted to live with him and have our happily ever after, but I couldn't just forget what happened before.

"One step at a time." I put my hand over his. "I need to go pack." I slowly pulled my hand away.

He sighed. "Fine. I suppose I have to let you go." He reached over and picked up his tea again. I put my tea down next to me and threw the duvet back. Before I could leave the bed, he pulled me back towards him. "But first, I want to ask you something." My lips parted. I was staring him in the eyes. I don't think I even blinked. "Freya, please be my girlfriend? My one and only?" He had a big smile on his face but in his eyes I could see just how nervous he was.

I didn't hesitate. I knew I wanted to be his girlfriend. "Of course!" I screamed. I moved over to his side and slowly moved to sit on top of him.

"Well, hello," he said in a husky voice. He placed his cup once more on the bedside table. He wrapped his arms around my waist and pulled me into his embrace. "Did you not want to think about your answer?" he teased.

I shook my head, smirking. I placed both hands on either side of his face, moving my face closer to his. I stopped just as our lips were about to meet. I steadied my breath and watched him; I could see his heart beating in his chest. It made me nervous.

Keeping my hands where they were, I moved closer into him and kissed him. I could feel him getting hard. I pulled away and gently bit his lip which made him groan.

"Tut tut, Miss Greene." He smirked. He put his right hand round the back of my head and pulled me back in. I slowly dropped my hands from his face and held onto the thin bedsheet that was in between my legs, between us. I lifted myself off him and tugged the bedsheet away. I grinned as I saw all of him. I then slowly sat back down and gasped as I felt him in between my legs. I started thrusting my hips back and forth ever so slowly, just so I could tease him, and also to show him how ready I was. I shuffled and lifted myself slightly once more as I re-positioned myself and him. I lowered myself back onto him, and this time, took him all in. The pleasure in feeling him fill me was exquisite. I moaned out as he hit me deep. I started to thrust my hips faster against him. He pushed his t-shirt that I was wearing slightly up so he could put both hands onto my hips. He opened his legs so he hit me deeper and moved with me easier. Every time I thrust my hips forward, he met my movement, sending a ripple crashing through my body. My lips met his, my tongue caressing and mirroring my rhythm. I liked being in control. I liked watching him fall apart beneath me.

I could tell he was getting close as his breathing

changed. With my next thrust forward, I started circling my hips slowly. He inhaled deeply through his teeth as I continued. My climb had started and so had his. He reached up to kiss me, but I shook my head and pulled away. I wanted to watch him. His grip tightened around my waist as he forcefully thrust his hips up hitting, my sweet spot deep, deep inside. Just like that, he took back control. He continued this harsh momentum as he started to moan. I wanted to take the control back. but I couldn't. My peak was near and I needed to explode around him. Just as I thought we were ready, he lifted me off him and put me on all fours. He pushed my back down so my bum and hips were in the air and my head, chest, and arms were down. He parted my legs a bit more as he smashed himself into me. He was hitting me even deeper than before. I couldn't hold on anymore, and neither could he. I screamed out his name as I came hard around him, as he did the same. He placed his hands on my hips to steady me; my legs were trembling.

"What a wonderful way to start the morning," he whispered before spanking me right on my arse cheek.

I stepped out of the shower and wrapped my hair in a towel. I really needed to get a shift on. I entered the bedroom to see naked Carter lying on his belly, his perfectly peachy bum showing slightly where the sheet had slid down. He took his eyes off his phone and looked over at me, flashing his gorgeous smile, followed by a wink. He made my insides melt.

I shook my head at him. "Not now, Mr Cole. You've had enough. I need to pack. I have a job and a life to go back to – I'm not rich like you." I scowled at him.

He rolled over, pulling the sheet with him. "Oh, you will be one day. You will be rich beyond your means." I stared at him. *Rich beyond my means. Shit.* I turned away and chose to ignore it. I rough dried my hair, slipped my jeans on, and pulled my t-shirt over my head. I walked over to the bed and leaned down to kiss him. Just as our lips touched, he pulled me on top of him.

"No!" I screamed, laughing. "Let me go. I need to go!"

He laughed and couldn't stop. I stopped struggling just to watch him.

"What are you staring at?" he teased.

I pulled myself away and sat on the edge of the bed. "You," I said, smiling. "I love watching you happy and laughing." I leaned down and kissed him. "Bye. I will see you when you're home." I got up off the bed. "Whenever that will be." I rolled my eyes. I heard him say something but, by the time I was at the door, it just sounded like a mutter. I walked quickly down the hall and into my room.

"Oh, you've returned." Courtney turned to face me.

"Yup, here I am." I smiled at her. "How did it go with Jude?"

A smile spread across her face. "We got him!"

"Ah, that's fantastic news! I bet Morgan is over the

moon," I said, matching her smile. This meant more work for me, but a much happier Morgan, hopefully.

She nodded. "He is really happy. He's a bit pissed that you weren't there, but I'm sure it will be fine." She turned around quickly and carried on packing her case.

"What do you mean *you're sure it will be fine*? Courtney, have I got something to worry about? You were going to cover for me and tell him I was ill!" I raised my voice.

She spun around and scowled. "I did cover for you!" she shouted. "He just isn't that stupid. He knew Carter was going to be here. He knew you would end up going back to him!" She sighed. "He hasn't said anything bad, Freya. I'm just warning you." She walked over to me. "I would have done the same." She gave me a weak smile and rested her right hand on the top of my arm. "Now, get packing. We leave in thirty minutes." She walked back over to her suitcase and continued to fold her clothes for her case. We packed in silence for a few moments when Courtney said, "So, me and Morgan are going official when we get home."

I couldn't hide my shock. "Really? His divorce hasn't even gone through yet and you two are going official?"

She scowled. "Yes. We're going official. We don't care about the divorce details and we don't care about what people think!" she said abruptly, looking me up and down before turning her nose up at me.

Oh, so she wants to be a bitch today.

"So long as you don't get hurt, then I'm really happy for you both." I stood next to her and wrapped my arm around her shoulders. "I really am." I gave her a little nudge and she smiled a little.

"So, how did it go with Carter? Was it worth risking your job for?" she said, winking at me.

"It was amazing. We spoke, we chilled, and honestly, we had the most amazing make up sex. My legs still feel like jelly now." I laughed as she blushed. "Ooh, have I made you uncomfortable, Court?" I elbowed her.

"No! Just now all I can picture is you and Carter having hot sex." She shook her head, closing her eyes at the same time, like she was trying to get the mental image out of her head.

"Oh, it was hot sex," I said, biting my lip, thinking back to our little moment that morning. "Anyway, did you have a good night with Morgan?" I asked her, and she was still blushing. "Yeah, it was nice. We had dinner, a few drinks and, of course, some dirty sex."

I raised my eyebrows. "Dirty sex?"

"Yup. A few toys, a bit of tying up and blindfolding. A bit of spanking and that." She turned a crimson red.

"Oh, like Fifty Shades dirty?" I teased. "Well, Court, I didn't realise you had it in you." She was still blushing. "We need a dinner date. I need the details." I really should have stopped but it was too good of a moment to pass up, especially when I never saw that side to Courtney.

I threw my last few items in my case and did it up. I checked my Louis Vuitton for my passport and phone charger; didn't want to leave them behind. I walked round to my side of the bed just to check the bedside drawers when I heard a knock at our hotel door. I looked up as Courtney opened it, and there he was, my beautiful Carter.

"Morning, Courtney." He smiled at her. She stood in silence, gawping up at him.

I walked quickly over to him and gave him a kiss on the cheek. "What are you doing here? We're leaving in ten." I looked at the time on my phone before shoving it in my pocket.

"I wanted to come and say goodbye. I'm on a later flight. My plane is here, but due to the amount of flights out today, we can't get a slot until later on." He sighed. "Which means it will be a few hours before I get to see you again. He wrapped his arms around my waist and pulled me in close, nuzzling into my neck. He pulled away as he saw Morgan approaching.

"Morgan," he said, in a deep, blunt voice

"Carter."

I looked over my shoulder at Courtney; she looked as awkward as me.

"I just overheard you saying your plane can't get a slot until later on, is that right?" he asked Carter.

"Yes, unfortunately."

"Well, I have space on my plane if you wanted to jump

on. "He smiled at Carter as they both un-tensed their shoulders

"Only if you're sure. It would make my life a little easier." Carter laughed.

"Of course. Not a problem." He stepped towards Carter and shook his hand. Morgan then walked towards Courtney. "We're leaving in five." He reached up and planted a lingering kiss on her forehead. "See you in a mo." He winked at her before walking back towards the hotel door. "Nice to see you smiling again, Freya," he said politely as he walked past me and Carter and down the hallway back to his room.

I finally let my held breath out. That was awkward. I looked over at Courtney who was doing the same.

We were both thinking the same thing; what a fun flight this was going to be.

CHAPTER SIXTEEN

We stood in the hotel lobby, waiting for Morgan and Carter to finish checking us out.

"Do you feel weird? You know, with those two being so friendly to each other, even though they are the biggest rivals?" I asked Courtney.

"A little bit. They will have to get used to it though. I'm not going to stop seeing you so they will have to deal with it." She smiled at me.

They both walked over, laughing. Morgan stood by Courtney's side and wrapped his arms around her. Carter stood by my side and kissed the side of my head, smelling my hair as he did.

"Our car is outside," Morgan said as he took Courtney's hand and started walking, Carter and I following.

"I can't wait to get home. Back to normality." I smiled up at him, squeezing his hand as I did.

We were finally on the plane after a nightmare at check

in. Courtney and Morgan snuggled up to each other. It was so nice seeing them together. They made such a lovely couple. Carter had his left hand in between my thighs, the right one resting on his leg. I had my arm wrapped through his.

"Let's go home," he said as the plane took off.

We landed back in rainy London. Luckily, we didn't have to wait for our luggage as we only had carry on. Morgan gave Courtney and me the rest of the day off work. We said our goodbyes at the airport. Carter's car was waiting outside, as was Morgan's.

I gave Courtney a cuddle. "See you tomorrow." I smiled at her.

"See you tomorrow. Enjoy your afternoon." She smiled back at me. I waved at Morgan. "Bye!"

We walked over to Carter's car; I was happy to see James.

"Freya." He smiled as he opened the door for me.

"Hey, James." I smiled back at him as I slid into the back of the car, and Carter followed me in.

"I'm looking forward to some alone time with you. Come back to the penthouse with me," he said. "Please."

"I can't." I shook my head, looking at the floor. "I have to get ready for work tomorrow, I have washing to do, and I need to get Tilly from Erin."

He put his finger up to my lips. "Shh. I will come back to yours then. I don't want to spend a moment away from

160

you." He smiled.

"It's a mess at my place. No food in, either. You know what I'm like." I nudged into him.

"We will stop at the shops and pick some food up. I'll cook."

"Oh, Carter. You don't have to do that."

"I want to."

"Then we can make the most of our evening." He winked at me.

My insides squirmed at the thought. I couldn't get enough of him. I didn't want dinner, I just wanted to skip straight to the after part.

"Can't wait." I bit my lip. He squeezed my knee and smiled.

We sat quietly, taking everything in. How mad had the last forty-eight hours been? I heard my phone beep. It was Laura. *Pfft.* I closed her message.

"You not going to reply?" He smirked at me.

"No. Not yet. Let her stew. She knows what she's done. I'm glad she intervened, obviously," I said, winking at him. "But she has pissed me off."

I also saw a voicemail from my mum that I had obviously missed:

Hello love, it's me, Mum. I hope you're enjoying Paris and have had a much-needed break. Come and see us soon, we miss you. Love you loads. Harry, say bye, dear. 'Bye babyface'. Ok then, bye. Love you.

I laughed. Oh, I did miss them.

"I'm going down to see my mum and dad soon. Wanna come?" I asked.

"Hmm, are you sure? Look what happened last time."

"Well, Mr Cole, that wouldn't have happened if you told me the truth from the start now, would it?" I replied bitterly.

"Now, now. That's all in the past. But, yes, I would love to come again. I feel like I need a weekend away already."

"Oh, stop it."

He started tapping away on his phone, replying to an email, sighing as he typed.

"What's wrong?" I asked.

"Nothing, babe. Just these arseholes in New York, now deciding to change the deal." He shook his head. "Does my head in. All of that for them to now start negotiating just as the paperwork is due to be signed."

I leaned over and kissed him on the cheek. "Try and forget about it. I don't want it to ruin our night." I smiled at him.

Carter leaned forward. "James, can you stop at the shops by Freya's flat, please? I need to grab some bits."

James looked in the rear-view mirror at Carter. "Sir, Julia has been out today and done your shopping."

Carter laughed and shook his head. "It's not for me, it's for Freya. Thank you." He sat back in his chair and placed his hand on my thigh, staring deep into my eyes.

We pulled up outside the little shop on the corner of the road where my flat was. Even though I'd only been gone for a few days, I felt like I'd been gone for weeks.

James opened the door as I stepped out, Carter right behind me. We walked around the shop.

"Anything you fancy in particular?" I asked Carter, while I was staring at the shelves.

"You."

I blushed. Oh, I couldn't wait to get him home. "No, seriously. What do you fancy?"

"What about pasta? Prawns, lemon, chilli with linguine?" My mouth started watering at the thought. "It's nice and light so we won't be bloated." He winked at me. I followed Carter as he walked to the wine chiller. "There isn't much of a selection. Happy with a Sauvignon?"

"Perfect. It's alcohol. You know me, I'm not fussy." I giggled.

"Come on. Let's get home. It's gone five p.m. already."

Carter paid for our dinner and jumped back into the car, James greeting us again.

"We could have just walked. It's only a ten minute walk," I said, annoyed.

"You're right, we could have, but I didn't want to," he said, smirking.

"Idiot." I shook my head.

We pulled up outside my block of flats. Ah, home, sweet home. I smiled as I looked at the building.

"Thank you, James. I will call you in the morning. Enjoy your night off." Carter shook James' hand.

James smiled at me. "Goodnight, Freya."

"Goodnight, James." I nodded at him and followed Carter into the block.

I walked past him on the stairs and unlocked my front door. I took a deep breath as I walked through. Carter put the bags on the worktop. I was in the bedroom, putting my suitcase down, when I felt arms around me, his big hands running around to my stomach and kissing my neck.

I smiled. "Hey, steady on. You promised me dinner, and I'm starved."

He moved away and turned me around. "Of course, my lady," he teased.

He walked into the kitchen and started unpacking our food. He poured me a glass of wine and handed it to me. I sat at the breakfast bar, watching him. I took a big mouthful of wine. Oh, it was good.

He started boiling the linguine. He sliced the lemons and peeled and butterflied the prawns. I watched his every move. For someone who had probably had cooks and housekeepers for most of his life, he knew how to cook.

"How hot do you like it?" Carter turned to face me, throwing me a subtle smirk.

"Oh, I like it very hot, Mr Cole." It came out of my mouth before I could think about it.

"We will see how hot you like it after dinner. Now, back

to my question. How hot do you want your pasta?"

"Just a few chilis, please. Don't want my tongue to catch alight."

"Dinner will be done in five. Pour me a glass of wine, please, and make some room at the breakfast bar for me."

I slid off the stool, tidied the old letters and magazines, and put them on top of my microwave. I walked over to the fridge and took the bottle out then poured him a glass. I sat back on the stool as Carter served up my pasta; it smelled divine. He squeezed some lemon over the top and gave me a knife and fork. "Enjoy." He beamed at me.

He came and sat next to me and took a mouthful of wine before tucking into his dinner.

"Oh. I am good. I am so good," he boasted.

"All right, pipe down, Gordon Ramsay." I chuckled, and he joined in with my laughter. He was right though; it was delicious.

I cleaned our plates away and tidied the kitchen. Carter had gone for a shower. I left the kitchen and turned the light off. I had text Erin when I got home to tell her I would get Tilly in the morning. I walked into the bedroom and saw Carter's clothes laid out on his bed. He was so neat compared to me. He must have hated it in my cluttered, messy flat.

I slipped my clothes off and let my hair down. I stood naked in front of the bathroom door for a few moments, took a deep breath, and opened the door.

I watched for a few seconds as Carter rinsed his hair off. I pulled back the shower curtain and stepped in. I wrapped my arms around him from behind and started planting kisses across his shoulders. I stood on my tiptoes as I kissed along his neck. I felt him relax as I continued planting kisses over his wet skin. He turned around and cradled my face, pulling me under the water with him. I placed my hands on his forearms to steady myself. He kissed me softly on my lips, still with his hands either side of my face. His tongue entered my mouth slowly, teasing mine. I opened my eyes to look at him, completely lost in the moment. He must have felt me looking at him as he opened his eyes too, trying not to smile. I closed my eyes as his kiss got hungrier. His tongue was a lot more forceful now as I matched his movements. I released my hands from his arms and ran them down his body, stopping just before I got to his groin. I slowly moved my finger down to his manhood and took it into my hand. He was so ready; I could feel his arousal on my fingertips. I started to move my hand up and down his thick, long shaft. I wanted him. But we only had the one wall to lean up against because of having an over bath shower. He bit my lip as I continued to pleasure him, moving slightly faster and tightening my grip around him. He moaned, throwing his head back then grabbing my jaw with his free hand and kissing me hard, no tongues this time. I loved watching him caught up in the moment, in the heat. The sex was always amazing, but every time, it got that little bit better. He released my jaw and grabbed my hand, signalling me to stop. He caught his breath and stepped out over the bath, taking my hand. I followed.

We stood on the bath mat, staring at each other. He gestured for me to lift my leg on the bath edge, while leaving the other foot on the floor. He smiled down at me. I knew that look. He moved down onto his knees and covered my sex with his mouth, slowly introducing his tongue against my sweet spot. I had one hand on the sink, the other had a handful of his hair, and I looked down and watched him. *Oh my.* It was such a turn on watching him, watching him bring me to life once more. Sending my body to her sweet release.

We walked into the bedroom. Just as I was about to throw a towel around me, he picked me up. I wrapped my legs around him. He pushed me up against the bedroom wall, thrusting into me. I gasped as he slowly moved. I dug my nails into the top of his back as he kept hitting me with the slow and tantalizing rhythm. I knew we wouldn't last long; we were caught up in the moment. His thrusts were getting deeper and faster as he was getting close. He squeezed my bum and buried his head into my neck as he hit his peak then sent me to my climax as I came hard, moaning his name. He carried me to the bed and dropped me onto it. He collapsed next to me.

"Satisfied, Miss Greene?" He grinned.

"Always, Mr Cole." I grinned back.

"I'm exhausted. I need a good night's sleep," he

muttered. "I couldn't sleep when we were apart. Now you're back, I feel so much more relaxed."

"Me too." I rolled over and kissed him on the forehead. "I'm just going to lock up." I crawled off the bed and threw his dirty t-shirt on. I just loved the smell of him. I walked down the hallway and locked the door.

"Hey, do you want a glass of water?" I shouted out from the kitchen, but got no response. I walked back into the bedroom and stood leaning against the doorframe. There he was, tucked up in bed, snoring. I smiled, feeling content and relaxed.

I tiptoed back into the kitchen and poured myself a drink. I turned the lights off once more and headed back to my room. I put my phone on charge and my drink on my bedside unit and climbed in next to him.

I watched him sleep for a few minutes; I just loved how peaceful he was, and how handsome he was. I really was a lucky girl.

I kissed him one last time on the lips, ever so gently, and lay down. I closed my eyes for a few seconds, opening them again to look at him, and smiled to myself.

I finally had my Carter back, and I was going to make sure I never let him go again.

CHAPTER SEVENTEEN

I was woken by Carter kissing me. "I've got to go, baby. Big meeting with these idiots from New York." He grunted.

I stretched. "Oh, back to reality," I mumbled.

"I know. It sucks." He smiled. "But I promise, in a few weeks, we will have a weekend break. Just me and you." He stood from the bed.

"That would be perfect." I smiled at him. "Have a good day."

"You too. I'll call you later. We really need to sort out our living arrangements. Think about it, please." He winked at me, his sage eyes twinkling. "Bye, baby," he said as he walked out the door.

"Bye!" I shouted back. I heard him shut the door. I didn't even know what the time was. I looked at my phone. six a.m. *Ugh.*

I lay in bed and for a few moments, thinking about what Carter said. *I could live with him. We know we want to be together, so what's stopping us?* I didn't have to be out of bed until at least seven, so I pulled the duvet up around my chin and watched a bit of TV.

At seven, I grabbed my phone and dialled Laura's number. *Let's hope she's up.*

"Hey!" She sounded happy to hear from me.

"Hello," I said bluntly.

"Erm, what's wrong?"

"Oh, I don't know, Lau. Was there something you forgot to mention about Paris?"

The phone went quiet. *Ha!*

"Freya, I was only trying to help, you know that, right?" I didn't reply. "If I told you that Carter was going, you wouldn't have gone. He reached out to me a few times and I ignored him. Then he asked if you were going Paris and I thought it would work out perfectly. He begged me to tell him."

"Why couldn't you just tell me? Why did it take me bumping into him and him telling me what you had arranged?"

"Because if I'd told you, you wouldn't have gone."

I sighed. "No."

"Exactly." I could hear the smile in her voice. "So, you saw him then."

"Yes. I also saw his girlfriend. I felt humiliated."

"I didn't know he had a girlfriend. Honestly."

"Yeah, well, it doesn't matter. He came home with me that night and we have been inseparable ever since." This time it was me who had the smile.

"Oh my God! Really? Oh, Freya. I'm so happy for you!"

"Slow down. It's only been a couple of days. He wants us to live together. It's all going a bit too fast for me."

"I know, but you do want to be with him, don't you? So what's really stopping you? Keep the flat, see how it goes. If it doesn't work or you need some time out, you still have your flat to go back to, don't you?"

"I suppose. I will talk to him tonight after work. How are you feeling, anyway?"

"Yeah, okay. Sickness has come back, so I've been signed off work for two weeks which is annoying, but it's best for the baby."

"Well, it's only a few weeks and you will be back at work. I can't wait to see you. I can't believe you're four months already. I also can't believe you didn't tell me until now!"

"It was nothing personal. I had a lot of sickness. I bled at the beginning so we just wanted to make sure everything was okay before we announced anything," she said quietly.

"I understand. I just can't wait to meet her. Anyway, hun, I better shoot. I've got to get ready. Don't want to be late. Let me know when you're free. I miss your face." I smiled.

"I miss you too. Love you."

"Love you."

I pressed the red button and dropped my phone beside

me. I really didn't want to get up.

I dragged myself out of bed and showered. I put my hair into a messy bun and raided my wardrobe. I really needed to do a shop for some new work clothes. I pulled out my favourite leather-look pencil skirt and a white, sleeveless, ruffle chiffon shirt. That would do.

I went to my underwear drawer and chose a black laced thong and white lace balcony bra. I slipped them on and got dressed. I'd just finished tucking my shirt into my skirt when there was a knock at the door.

"Coming!" I shouted out as I ran out of the bedroom. I swung the door open to find a young girl with a beautiful bouquet of flowers. I blushed and took the flowers from her. "Thank you." I smiled as I shut the door.

A dozen red roses. They were beautiful. I put them on my worktop and opened the card:

"They say you only fall in love once, but that can't be true... Every time I look at you, I fall in love all over again."

I swooned, a beaming smile spreading across my face. Oh, I loved him. I popped the card back in the flowers and went back into my bedroom to finish getting ready.

I walked in the office doors and said good morning to the security guard. He wasn't as friendly as the ones I used to work with at Jools' offices. I stepped into the lift and headed up to my office. I walked in and saw Courtney sitting at her desk. She waved eagerly at me. I smiled and nodded.

Morgan was sitting in his office, hiding behind his computer screen. I slid into my seat and switched my computer on. I looked up and Courtney had gone from her desk. I loaded up my emails and sighed as they all downloaded. It was going to be a busy Tuesday.

Within a few minutes, Courtney popped up beside my desk. "Here you go." She smiled, passing me a cup of coffee.

"Thank you, love."

She walked away and sat back at her desk, tapping away on her computer. I picked my coffee up and took a big mouthful.

I had a scroll up and down on the computer, deciding which email to tackle first. I clicked on a submission that had come in that caught my eye, when Morgan called me in. I stood up and walked into his office.

"Hey. Everything okay?" I asked cautiously. He was so different out of work than in.

"Morning, Freya. Please take a seat." He smiled and gestured for me to sit down. I did as he asked. "So, as you may be aware, the signing with Jude Prior went amazingly. He wants us to publish his book which is fantastic for us."

"That is fantastic!" I beamed.

"Yes, it is. I need you to start working on the contracts, please. There is a lot he is asking for, so we need to really read through everything to make sure we meet every need. I don't want this to fuck up," he said sternly.

"Of course. I will get started right away. I was just

173

going through my emails as there was quite a bit that needed to be answered."

"Pass them to Courtney. She is your assistant, after all," he said bluntly.

Oh, how I despise work Morgan.

"Perfect. I will do that now," I said, standing up slowly. "Is there anything else?"

"Don't fucking mention anything to Carter. I don't want him to know until he needs to," he snapped.

I nodded and walked out of his office. He was such a bastard.

I sat back down at my desk and typed an email to Courtney:

From:Freya.Greene@lornesandhucks.co.uk
To:Courtney.Strand@lornesandhucks.co.uk

Subject: Sorry!

Hey doll,

Sorry, but I have been instructed to forward all 157 emails to you for you to deal with. I've got to work on the contract for Jude Prior.

I will treat you to lunch, I promise.

I'll start forwarding them now.

XX

Freya Greene
Assistant Editor to Morgan Lornes
Lornes and Hucks Publishing

I sighed as I started sending her the emails. I saw her eyes burning into me over her computer screen.

I stretched in my seat and looked at the time. One-thirty already. I was starving. I locked my computer screen and slipped my shoes back on. I checked my phone and had a couple of messages from Carter. One agreeing to pick me up, one telling me what he was going to do to me. I blushed.

I picked my bag up and walked out of the office. I'd missed my little bistro. I popped into the little bakery opposite the office and got a ham salad sandwich and some water. I had a caffeine headache.

I rushed back to my desk and ate my lunch there; I really didn't want to piss Morgan off anymore. I finished my sandwich and took a massive mouthful of water before losing myself in my work.

The office started quieting down; I was exhausted.

I really wanted to go home, but I needed to get this done. Courtney came over. "Hey, it's four. Are you not leaving?"

I looked up from my computer screen. "Unfortunately not. I need to get this finished before Morgan has my arse." She threw me a look. "Not literally!"

She huffed. "Just don't work too late. See you tomorrow." She leaned down and kissed me on the cheek.

"I won't. Bye, hun." I smiled at her

My phone started buzzing. It was Carter. "Hey you." I smiled.

"Hey, beautiful. I'm downstairs. You ready?"

"I wish. I have about half an hour left of work. Are you okay to wait? Please?"

I heard him sigh then let out a little laugh. "I'll wait. Don't be long, or I'll come in there and take you," he said sternly.

"Okay, okay. Love you." It slipped out.

"I love you too," he replied.

I was finishing my last section when I heard the office door open. I turned around to see Carter. It was six p.m.

"Oh my God. I'm so sorry. I'm on my last section!" I said apologetically.

"I'm hungry," he moaned.

"So am I. I promise I'm nearly done. I really don't want to piss Morgan off."

"Why would you piss him off?"

"Because he wants this contract done by tomorrow. Sorry, I've been told not to discuss it with you." I smirked at him, knowing it was going to annoy him.

He ran his hand through his tousled hair. "Did he now?" he said, coming closer to me, his eyes burning into mine.

"What is going through your head, Mr Cole?" I teased.

"Oh, you don't want to know." He smirked and leaned down and kissed me. "As much as I want to take my frustration out on you here, especially on Morgan's desk, I just want to get you home. I want to eat dinner with you and then take my time on you," he whispered. "Now, hurry up. This man needs food." He stepped away and put his hands in his pockets, walking around, looking at Morgan's office. "You're wasted here," he mumbled. "Come back and work for me."

I laughed. "No way. Not yet, anyway. One step at a time." I winked at him. "Now, please, be quiet. I'm nearly finished."

I sat in the car and sighed with relief. "I'm so glad to be out of the office. Morgan is so different to work with. I feel sorry for Courtney, having to deal with him in that mood."

"All the more reason for you to leave." He smirked

"Carter…" I warned. He rolled his eyes at me. "What's for dinner?" I asked. I was so hungry.

"Julia is preparing a roast. I was craving one. She cooks the best roast potatoes." He smiled fondly.

"I can't wait to try them. Love a roastie." I smiled.

We pulled up outside the penthouse. I was nervous. I much preferred his townhouse; it was homelier. James let us out of the car and saw us into the building. As we walked through the front door, the smell of roast beef filled my nostrils. My belly rumbled even more. Carter dismissed

James and he wished us both goodnight. I watched as he walked upstairs and disappeared into his room.

"Evening, Mr Cole, Miss Greene. Dinner will be ready in ten," Julia said chirpily. She was a very slim lady with black hair, blue eyes, and pale skin. She must have been mid-thirties. She had a wedding band on. I wondered how her husband coped with her being a live-in housekeeper, unless her husband was there as well.

"Thank you, Julia." Carter smiled warmly at her. He seemed very fond of her.

We sat down at the dining room table. I couldn't wait to get changed.

"My mum and Ava are coming down in a few weeks. I would love for you to spend the weekend here. Maybe invite your mum and dad down. It would be nice for them to finally meet." He smiled at me.

"That would be lovely. I'll check with my parents." I returned his smile.

Julia walked over and served our dinner. I felt weird being waited on.

"Thank you. It looks and smells delicious," I said.

We sat on the sofa with a glass of red, the fire roaring, French doors pulled to. Carter was wearing his jogging bottoms and a t-shirt, and I was wearing a tracksuit he had bought. It was nice being out of my skirt; I felt so bloated. I ate too much. *Story of your life,* my subconscious snarled.

"I've been thinking about what you said, about moving

in." I tapped my nails on my glass anxiously.

His eyes lit up. "Really?"

"Yes, really."

He leaned across the sofa and kissed me passionately. "This is great!" he exclaimed as he pulled away. "Will you move in here?"

"At the moment, yes, but honestly, Carter, I would like us to buy somewhere. Somewhere new." I looked up at him.

"Of course. I completely understand. Let's take our time and find our perfect home." He scooted closer to me and kissed me once more.

"Look, there's something I want to talk to you about," I said quietly. He looked at me, his eyebrows furrowed, his eyes watching mine. "Don't be worried. It's not bad," I reassured him. "Go pour us another glass of wine, then we can talk."

He smiled and walked over to the kitchen to grab the bottle.

CHAPTER EIGHTEEN

Carter sat next to me, placing a bottle of red on the coffee table. He rubbed his hands anxiously. His eyes were wide with worry. It was hard to watch him when he was like that. It was like he lost all trust.

"Look, I just wanted to say sorry for the way I acted when everything came out. You know, back in Elsworth." I cleared my throat. Carter opened his mouth to speak. "No, shh." I pressed my finger against his lips. "My turn to talk." I smiled weakly. "If we're going to move forward in this relationship, I need to get this off my chest." He sat silent, waiting. I knotted my fingers. "I should have followed you. I should have ignored everything and everyone and got in the car." I looked down at my fingers and sighed. "Watching you drive away was like no other pain I had ever felt. My heart broke. I was trying to be strong, to prove a point to myself. I really don't know why. I should have just picked up the phone and called you, except I deleted and blocked your number. I shouldn't have let you go. The moment I did,

I broke my own heart. I just didn't know how much I loved you, how much I needed you." My eyes started welling up as I looked at his face for a reaction. A single tear escaped, running down his face. "I'm sorry," I whispered.

I blinked as my tears began to fall. He scooped me up into an embrace, covering my mouth with his. Our kiss was raw and full of emotion. Anger, hurt, and love. He pulled me onto his lap as we continued to kiss, neither of us wanting to stop.

He pulled away, looking at me, wiping my tears. "I shouldn't have driven away. I should have been more determined. I knew where you lived, where you worked, yet I hid behind a phone," he choked. "Freya, this is it. Me and you. No fucking up this time." He sighed, returning to kiss me. "I love you so much."

"I love you too." I smiled.

"Come on. Let's go to bed. I'm exhausted," he said, lifting me off him. He then took my hand and led me to the bedroom.

A few weeks had passed, work was booming. Morgan was happy now Jude Prior was officially ours. Still hard work, but a lot happier.

I logged onto my computer and opened my emails; I had a few submissions to go through. I loved reading authors' work.

I heard my phone beep, I looked and smiled. It was

Carter:

Hurry home Miss Green, I miss you X

I huffed. All right for some. Working from home, our home. Things were going well with us living together. It was hard adjusting, having everyone do something for me. I wanted to tell them to let me help, but I didn't dare.

Courtney interrupted me. "Coffee?" she asked. "You look knackered. Has Carter been keeping you awake at night?"

"Hey. Coffee would be lovely, thank you. I wish. I can't keep my eyes opened past nine p.m. at the moment!" I smiled

"Are you okay?"

"Of course. It's just been so hectic with the move and work. I feel like I'm getting a bit of a cold. I'm glad it's Friday night." I sighed. "What have you got planned for this weekend?"

"Not a lot. Out tonight, then spending the rest of weekend with Morgan. Between you and me, his divorce is finalized." She beamed, excited. "We can finally move on with our relationship."

"I'm so happy for you both. Maybe we should get a date night in. Let them talk about work, and we can drink," I suggested.

"That would be lovely. I will check Morgan's diary and send you some dates!" She waved and walked into the kitchen.

A few moments later, I had a hot coffee in my hand. I took a breather for a couple of minutes as I enjoyed a bit of quiet. I took a sip and smiled. Courtney knew how to make a good coffee. I placed my cup back down and smiled as I looked at the picture of Carter and me on my desk; he was so handsome. I tore my eyes away and started typing my recommended authors to Carla. I stopped typing as my stomach turned, and I panicked. I was going to be sick. I looked around me; I wouldn't make it to the toilets in time. I picked up my bin and threw up. I reached out and grabbed the tissue that was being held in front of me. *Oh, Courtney.* I wiped my eyes that were streaming from the heaving. I looked up and saw the whole office staring at me. I smiled weakly at them and slowly put the bin down. I looked at my coffee and was instantly put off. Courtney returned with a glass of water. "Here," she said as she placed it in my hands. "Drink up."

"Thank you," I said quietly. My voice seemed to have gone. I took a few little sips.

"You feeling better now? Norovirus is going around," she said sympathetically. "Always seems to come around the end of October." She rubbed my shoulder with her hand. I just nodded and wiped my eyes again. "Freya, go home. It's not worth being here. If it is a bug, you'll wipe us all out. It's Friday, anyway. I'll tell Morgan. A weekend full of rest will do you the world of good."

"Thank you, hun. Don't want to pass this bug onto any

of you." I logged my computer off and picked my bag up. I snuck out quietly; I had already caused a scene.

I stood outside the office, and the cool October air hit me. I started to feel queasy again. *Not now, please.* As soon as I thought it, I ran back into the lobby and straight into the toilets. I started to cry. I hated being sick. I heard a knock on the door; it was one of the security guards. "Freya, are you okay?" he asked.

I nodded. "Could you do me a favour, please..." I realised I didn't know his name.

"Jason." He smiled.

"Could you do me a favour, please, Jason?" I said as I stood up.

"Anything."

"Can you call my boyfriend for me? Tell him I'm sick and I need him to collect me ASAP. Sandra on the front desk has his details." Just as I finished, I started being sick again.

"Right away, Freya." He dashed out the door.

I sat hugging the toilet, eyes red raw from the crying and heaving, when I heard the door burst open.

"Freya!" I heard Carter's voice, frantic with worry. He walked around the corner and found me. "Oh, baby." He bent down and kissed my forehead. "Let's get you home," he whispered. He scooped me up effortlessly. He thanked Jason and Sandra as we walked through the lobby. James already had the car door open for us. He placed me down gently on the seat and slid in next to me. "Are you okay?" he asked, brows furrowed.

"No."

"Is it a bug?"

"I think so. It's being going around the office and now I've been struck with it," I wailed. I didn't cope very well being ill.

"Julia has run you a bath. Once you're done, straight to bed," he said sternly.

My stomach started churning again, but luckily, there was nothing left to come out.

I had never been so grateful to be home. Carter wouldn't let me walk, even though I insisted I was feeling better. I didn't argue with him. I was exhausted. He took me through to our bathroom that overlooked London. He stood me in front of the bath and undressed me. He took my hand to steady me as I stepped into the bath; the hot water felt amazing.

He took off his t-shirt, exposing his glorious body; I could have devoured him.

"I don't think so." He grinned at me, as if he had read my mind. I sulked as I slid down into the bath, wetting my hair. I sat up as he lathered me with soap, slowly pouring the warm water over me to wash it off. I smiled at him. "Thank you."

"You're most welcome." He kissed me on the cheek before lifting me out of the bath.

I was lying in our bed, watching *Friends*. I felt

famished. Carter was sitting on top of the covers, replying to emails.

"Babe," I said quietly.

"What's wrong?"

"Nothing. Could I have some toast? I'm so hungry." I gave him my best puppy dog eyes.

"You're meant to starve a bug." He frowned at me.

"It doesn't feel like a bug. It could have been something I ate. Tom bought some egg and sausage rolls in for breakfast. They did taste a bit funny."

He shot me a look. "And you still ate it?" he asked, disgusted.

"Babe, this is me. I don't turn down food." I elbowed him, giving him a big grin. "Now, please, some toast with butter." I shooed him out of the bed, my mouth watering at the thought of food.

Five minutes later, he returned with two slices of toast and a cup of tea. My tummy grumbled.

I took a small bite, and my taste buds exploded. Something so simple, yet so satisfying.

Carter sat next to me and returned to his emails. Once I had finished my toast, I wrapped my hands around my tea cup. My phone beeped. I reached over and checked – Courtney.

She was checking in. She was kind when she wanted to be. I sighed and put my phone down. I was bored. I put my cup next to my phone and started running my finger slowly up Carter's leg. He looked at me, shaking his head. I bit my lip, continuing to ignore him. I then ran two fingers up and down his thigh. As I came back up, I started stroking his already hard shaft. He breathed in. "Freya, you're meant to be resting." He looked down his nose at me.

"But I don't want to rest."

I slowly moved and climbed on top of him. I picked up his laptop and put it on the floor to the side of us. When I came back up and looked at Carter, I could see the want in his eyes. Before I could make my next move, he kissed me, nipping at my lip. He trailed his kisses down my neck and towards my collarbone, occasionally nipping my skin. I was wearing a black silk nightdress. Carter slipped his little finger under my shoulder straps and pulled them down my arms delicately. He took one of my breasts into his mouth and sucked it hard, causing a sensitive sting through my body. I gasped. I greedily tried to release him; I was so wanting for him, I was panting. I rested my hands on his shoulders as I lifted myself up, signalling for him to pull his trousers down. He threw his head back in defeat against our headboard as he gave in. He returned to my breast, sucking and nipping. His hands pushed my nightie up around my waist. I lifted my hips slightly as I guided him to where I wanted him to be. The deep, filling feeling overtook my senses. I felt like I was building quickly. I slowed down my thrusting; I didn't want it to be over, not yet. I stopped and leaned down to kiss him, his sage eyes open, watching my every move. Just as I started to calm myself down, he pushed me from on top of him, pinning my arms above my head with his hand. He used his other hand to push my thighs apart, exposing me. His fingers slowly entered me. With each thrust, he was brushing over my sweet spot. His face hovered over mine, his eyes watching mine. I started to moan again. He slowly pulled his fingers out and entered me, teasing me the whole time. I started to moan each time he pushed into me, and each time, he got harder. He reached down and started kissing my neck, his thrusting speeding up, hitting me deeper and deeper each time. I called out his name as I was getting near my peak. He leaned back down and whispered in my ear, "Come." With that, I came hard around him, with him following me.

"Now, you nympho. Can I get back to my work?" he said after our five-minute down time.

"Of course." I beamed. "I got what I wanted."

"Well played, Freya." He smiled.

"Now, seriously. Get some rest. You need to get better."

"Fine." I scowled. "I'm just going to get some water." I slipped out of bed and tiptoed into the kitchen; it was quiet. It was only five p.m. I walked over to the fridge and pulled out the big glass bottle of water. I stood on my tiptoes to reach the glasses then poured myself a drink. I stood in the kitchen, thinking about the last month. We had come so far. I was startled when I heard someone enter the kitchen. *Shit.* It was James, and I was dressed in my nighty.

"I'm so sorry, Freya! I didn't mean to startle you. Mr Cole dismissed us for the evening so I was just coming to get some snacks." He didn't know where to look.

"Don't be silly. It's fine. Enjoy your evening," I replied as I grabbed my glass and ran out of the kitchen. I snuck back into the room, flustered.

"You okay?" Carter asked. "Are you feeling sick again?"

"No. I, erm, I just bumped into James in the kitchen."

"Lucky James," he mumbled.

"You're not mad?"

"Why would I be mad? You're mine, I'm yours. James and the rest of this household know that so there's nothing to worry about." He patted the bed. "Time for rest."

I leaned over and kissed him once more. "You know how to treat a lady." I winked. "I'm very lucky to have you all to myself." I bit my lip and rolled over. As I did, he gave my bum a little slap.

I felt shattered again. Maybe a little half hour sleep would help. At least I wasn't feeling sick anymore. Bloody sickness bug. I just hoped Carter didn't get it.

CHAPTER NINETEEN

As I woke, I felt Carter snuggled into me. It was a cold morning; I didn't want to get out of bed. I looked at the clock. It was nine a.m. I felt so well rested but exhausted at the same time. I was so glad it was Saturday. We had plans to see Laura and Tyler but, at that moment, I wasn't leaving my bed. Carter was snoring softly, deep in sleep. I rolled over and watched him; there was something calming about watching him. I closed my eyes, trying to doze back off. I opened my eyes as I felt my mouth starting to water. I bolted out of bed and straight into the bathroom, once again throwing up. I wiped my eyes, stood up, and walked over to the basin to brush my teeth. I watched myself in the mirror when my toiletry unit caught my eye. I noticed my tampons. I dropped my toothbrush, mouth wide open.

I turned the tap off and wiped my mouth. I walked out of the bathroom and quietly sat on the edge of the bed, opening my bedside drawers, reaching for my pill packet. I slid the packet out of its holder and studied the days; I hadn't missed any. *What the hell?* I thought over and over. I was on the mini pill. I was one of the unlucky ones that still had a light period every month. I opened my period diary that I kept in my drawer along with my pills, and flicked back a couple of weeks. I gasped. There it was; my little star to remind me that my period was due. *Shit.* Panic set in. How the bloody hell had I not realised I had skipped my period? I threw my head in my hands, trying to calm my breathing. Maybe it was just stress that stopped it coming. I was trying to work out when I could have fallen if I was. It must have been the night we got back from Paris. That worked out about three weeks ago. I looked over my shoulder at Carter as he started to stir. I put my pills and diary back in my drawer and got back into bed. I laid there, eyes fixed on the ceiling, heart thumping out of my chest.

"Morning, beautiful." He smiled and kissed me on the cheek.

I turned to face him. "Morning, handsome." I smiled back as I received his kiss

"Sleep well?"

"Like a log." I beamed.

"You feeling better? You look a little washed out. Have you been sick again?"

"I have."

"Oh, baby," he said sympathetically. "I hate that you're ill." He kissed my forehead. "Hopefully the bug will be out of your system soon."

"I don't think it's a bug," I whispered, trying not to cry.

"What do you mean?" He sat up and cocked his head to the side, his sage eyes searching my face. I didn't look up, just watched my hands.

"I've skipped a period," I muttered. "I don't know how. I'm on the pill. I haven't skipped any; I take it the same time. Every. Single. Day." I emphasized the last three words. I threw my head back as the tears started rolling. Why now?

"You've not tested, have you?" He spoke quietly.

"No," I sobbed.

"Then don't worry yet. It could just be stress. I will send James out to grab a couple of tests. Please don't get upset. We can deal with it." He smiled and kissed my tears.

I smiled at him. "You are wonderful." I grabbed his hand and squeezed it tight.

"As are you." He squeezed my hand back as he got up. "I'm going to see James. You stay there. Try and rest." He smiled at me as he walked out the door.

I couldn't rest. My heart was thumping, my anxiety through the roof. I pulled the duvet up around my face and let out a little cry.

A few minutes later, Carter returned with cups of tea for us both. "James has just left. He should be back in about ten minutes." He smiled.

He walked over to my side of the bed and handed me my tea. "Thank you."

He came and sat next to me and rested his hand on my

leg. "It will be okay, Freya. Whatever the outcome. I promise." I nodded in agreement. "You haven't been to the toilet yet, have you? Only Julia said it's better with the first wee of the morning."

"Okay," I mumbled. I took a sip of my tea and sat back against the headboard. We didn't talk, just sat in silence waiting for James, Carter not letting go of my hand the whole time.

Twenty minutes had passed when there was a knock on the bedroom door. Carter jumped up and jogged to the door. He opened it slightly and took the bag from James.

"Thank you for that, James." He nodded and closed the door. He reached into the bag and put the two tests on the bed. "Come on. Let's go find out," he said hopefully.

I climbed out of bed and walked into the bathroom. Carter was reading the instructions while looking at the test, confused.

"Give it to me." I shook my head as I took the test from him. I took it out of its wrapper and sat on the toilet. Knowing Carter was there was making it impossible to go.

"I can't wee with you here," I said, embarrassed. "Can you just wait outside the door? Please?"

He nodded and walked just outside the bathroom. I read the instructions once more before taking the test. I called him back in as soon as I had done it. I placed it on the basin unit as I washed my hands. I didn't want to look at it. Carter walked over to me. I wrapped my arms around his waist and squeezed him, resting my head on his chest. I could feel his heart beating fast.

"Can we look yet?" he asked.

"It says wait three minutes," I said, still clinging onto him.

"Well, there is something on there already." He peeled my arms from around his waist and took my hand as we walked over.

I gasped. He squeezed my hand. There it was; a dark blue cross. I was pregnant.

I dropped Carter's hand and held onto the sink. I felt sick. Carter still stood looking at the test. I sobbed quietly. *How has this happened? Why has it happened?*

I watched as Carter's arms made their way around my waist, his hands resting on my stomach. I looked up in the mirror at him; he looked as scared as me.

"Baby, I promise we will get through this. Everything happens for a reason, remember?" I just stared at him. "We both wanted kids. We want to be together, and we love each other. We will just have another little person to focus on." He swallowed. "Honestly, this is the best news for me. I couldn't imagine not having kids with you. Yeah, okay, it happened a little earlier then we would have liked." He took a breath. "But it's happened. We are going to be parents, Freya. I love you." He turned me around and embraced me.

"I'm scared," I whispered through sobs.

"I know you are, and so am I," he whispered back. "But

we will be just fine, you know that, don't you?" I nodded. "I promise you, Freya. We will." He cradled my face, kissing me ever so softly. It was like his lips were feathers, brushing over mine. I kissed him back, a little more forcefully.

"Let's keep it quiet until we've had our scan. I'll call my doctor and get us booked in." He smiled. "I am so happy, baby." He rested his hand on my face and I leaned into it, resting my hand on top of his.

"I love you," I whispered, tears still in my eyes. I didn't want to blink as they would escape and I still hadn't worked out if they were happy tears or scared tears.

We kissed once more before leaving the bathroom. I snuck back into bed and put the TV on.

"I'm going to make you some breakfast, be back soon." He winked at me.

As he shut the door, I put my hands on my tummy and looked down.

"Hey you. Mummy is a bit shocked right now. But, I promise, me and Daddy will love you so fiercely. No one will ever love you like me and him." I smiled.

I grabbed my phone and asked if Laura was still up for meeting. I really wanted to tell her, but Carter was right. We needed to wait for our first scan.

I sent the message and put my phone back down just as Carter walked through the door. He came in with a little tray of food that smelled amazing.

He placed it on my lap; it was full of goodies. Fresh

orange juice, ham and cheese omelette, and a bowl full of strawberries, melon, and blueberries.

"Looks delicious," I said with a mouthful of fruit.

"Now we need to make sure you eat during the day. It's not just you now," he said, lying on his belly, resting his head in his hands.

He lay like that the whole time I ate my breakfast; he was like a dog waiting for a bit of food to be dropped. I pushed the tray away. I was so bloated.

"Freya, you've left half your omelette." He frowned.

"I'm full up. My tummy has probably shrunk from being sick." I frowned back at him.

"Fine."

He pushed me back so I was lying up against the headboard. He turned on his side and laid his ear on my tummy, looking at me the whole time. He looked so happy.

We had finally got out of bed and showered. I still felt bloated so decided on a loose fitted, long-sleeved dress from Zara with some thick black tights and heeled black ankle boots. It was cold out so I wanted to make sure I was warm, but most of all, comfortable.

Carter came out of the bathroom. He looked as handsome as ever. He finished running his hands through his hair with his wax to get his tousled look. He was wearing a grey roll neck jumper, fitted skinny dark blue jeans, chukka boots and a Harrington jacket. He sprayed some of his aftershave and walked over to me, kissing me on the cheek.

"You look as beautiful as ever," he mumbled in my ear as he stood behind me, wrapping his arms tightly around my waist. My hair was down and curly, my make-up natural, but I had a bit more bronzer on than normal. The sickness had taking the colour from my cheeks. Hopefully, it would calm down a bit now. I'd been sick five times that morning. I finished putting my earrings in as he nuzzled into my neck. "You smell divine."

"So do you." I looked over my shoulder at him and kissed him quickly, my lipstick lingering on his lips. "That's a good look for you," I teased.

"Yeah? I might rock this out to lunch. Bring it with you." He winked at me. I giggled. "Come on. We're going to be late," he said, walking over to his bedside unit and slipping his Rolex onto his wrist.

"Okay, okay. I'm ready. Let me just get my bag." I walked out of the dressing room, through the bathroom, and into the bedroom and picked up my bag. I walked quickly back through and met Carter in the dressing room.

"Right, let's go. James driving?" I asked as we left the dressing room which was attached to the bathroom.

"Not today. I am." He smiled. "I've given James the day off."

"That's nice of you." I smiled back at him.

He took my hand as we walked out of our home. I loved this man very much.

We walked into the underground car park towards Carter's spaces. I saw his Maserati. Last time I saw that, he was driving away from me. I touched my tummy. How things had changed. He walked straight past it and unlocked the Land Rover next to it.

"Oh, when did you get that?" I asked.

"A few months ago." He smiled smugly. "Good job I did, what with our little arrival coming into the world in a few months." He opened my door and took my bag as I got in; he was such a gentleman.

"Thank you."

"You're welcome." He closed the door gently.

The car was stunning; grey metallic paint with blacked out windows and black alloys. The inside was soft, stitched leather. I ran my fingers across the dashboard. "The car is lovely." I smiled at him.

"I'm glad you like it. It's yours." He looked at me with a big grin on his face.

"What?" I said, shocked. "Carter – I can't. Don't be silly." I shook my head.

"It's yours. I ordered it before we went Elsworth..." He stopped talking briefly and clenched his fist. "Anyway, it's yours."

"But..."

He shook his head. "No buts." He took my hand and kissed it. "Let's go see our friends. Love you, Miss Greene." He let go of my hand and started the engine.

198

"I love you too, Mr Cole."

I looked out of the window as we left the car park, the sun shining on that chilly October afternoon. I was nervous but excited to see Laura. I just hoped I could keep my food down when I was out. I pulled my sunglasses out of my bag and listened to the radio, placing my hand on Carter's thigh. He followed and rested his hand on mine and gave it a squeeze, smiling.

God knows how I was going to avoid drinking. Laura knew I loved a glass of wine, especially with my food. I would just say I was recovering from a sickness bug. I closed my eyes as Carter pulled onto the motorway, just for a few moments.

CHAPTER TWENTY

Thirty minutes later, we pulled up outside the restaurant. I hadn't been there before. It was a cosy little Italian just outside London. I do love Italian.

The porter took the keys from Carter and drove the car into the car park. He took my hand as we walked up the step. We were greeted by the host who showed us to our table. Laura and Tyler were already sitting there. Laura slid out of the table to reveal a tiny little bump; my heart hurt. We ran up to each other and cuddled. Tyler and Carter shook hands, wishing each other a good afternoon.

"OMG, Lau, look at you. You look blooming lovely." I beamed. "Pregnancy suits you." I stepped back and admired her.

"Thank you," she said, blushing. Her blonde hair was glossy and thick, her skin glowing.

"How are you? I ordered you a glass of wine. I have non-alcoholic. At least I can feel like I'm drinking." She laughed.

"Oh, thanks, hun, but I'm not drinking." I could feel Carter's eyes burning into me "I'm getting over a nasty bug so still trying to be careful on what I eat and drink." I smiled at her, then I saw her panic. "Oh, God, don't panic! I was ill at the beginning of the week. I'm fine now. Just don't want to risk it," I said as I slid into the booth next to Carter.

The waiter brought our drinks over. I declined my wine and asked for some water. He nodded and took my glass back. Carter picked up his pint and took a big mouthful.

"Oh, that tastes good," he teased, throwing me a look.

The waiter returned with my water and some menus. I was so hungry.

"So then," Laura said, clearing her throat. "So did you enjoy your weekend in Paris? I know we touched on it." She smirked

"Eventful." I laughed. "But so amazing." I beamed at Carter. "Still not happy that you knew he was going and didn't tell me." I scowled at her.

She sighed. "Like I said, if I had told you he was going, you never would have gone."

"She is right, Freya. You wouldn't have," Tyler piped up.

"Oh, and, Mr Cole, I heard you took a girlfriend with you," Laura quizzed.

He let out a low laugh. "That's right, but she knew what was going on. Like I said to Freya, she was just a fill gap until I got her back."

I rolled my eyes. "Very cocky, aren't you?"

"Very."

"Who made the first move?" Tyler asked, winking at Carter.

"Of course it was Carter. If he hadn't seen me, I would have run back to my hotel. I didn't want to see him." I winced. "As horrible as that sounds."

"Don't worry. I understand." He rubbed the back of my knuckles with his thumb.

"Did you have sex more than once the night you met?" Laura asked boldly. I spat my water out and into my lap. They all started laughing as Carter handed me a tissue.

"That's none of your business," I said abruptly

"We totally did. All night long." Carter chuckled then fist bumped Tyler as they laughed more.

"Ooh, you two." Laura winked at me.

"Anyway, enough about that. What are you eating?" I asked seriously, Carter and Tyler still chuckling. He was such a child, but I loved that they got on.

"Well, the baby doesn't like overly greasy food, so I might just go for a Bolognese or something," she said, studying the menu. The thought of that made my stomach turn. *Oh, God. Not now.* I took a sip of water, trying to push the thought away.

"Think I'm going to go for a pizza," Carter replied.

"Can I share with you? I'm not overly hungry," I said.

"Of course. You okay?" I looked at Laura and Tyler who

were deep in their menus. I shook my head. "Still haven't quite got my appetite back," I whispered.

"Okay, babe. I won't go for a heavy pizza. Something light." He smiled sympathetically at me.

The waiter returned to take our order. I sat and listened as they all ordered, sipping my water. I didn't want to panic Laura, but I felt rough. If I ran to the loo, she would think I still had the bug. I tried not to think about it, but it was easier said than done.

After struggling with my lunch, Laura started asking questions. "Are you okay? It's unlike you not to eat your food."

"I'm fine, it's just this bug has really taken my appetite away."

"You sure it's a bug?" I felt Carter's eyes on her. I sighed. I went to reply but Carter cut across me.

"She's pregnant," he said, throwing me a caring look.

"Oh my God." Laura dropped her fork and stared at me. "You're pregnant! How? When?"

Tyler shook his head. "Do you really need to know how? Do you not remember?" He laughed. "I know you claim to have 'baby brain'." He quoted 'baby brain' with his fingers. "But surely you haven't forgotten that night?"

"Why didn't you tell me?" Laura asked.

"That's rich coming from you."

Carter intervened. "To be honest, I told her not to tell anyone. I wanted us to get scanned, then make sure everything was okay after our twelve-week scan, which I'm sure you can understand seeing as you didn't tell Freya until you were four months," he said bluntly.

"Sorry, I'm just shocked. When did you find out?" she asked, still not taking her eyes off me.

I sighed again. "This morning. We're shocked too, Laura. It's not like we planned this, it just happened. We didn't want this just yet, but, we are over the moon." I smiled at Carter, and he was smiling too.

"Wow, it happened so quickly," she said, stunned. "Tyler and I have been trying for about a year, even before the wedding." She looked down, picked her fork up, and twirled her pasta. Tyler reached over and touched her hand. "Congratulations though. It's wonderful. At least our babies will be close." She half-smiled.

"That's true. They could be besties, just like us." I reached across and took her other hand, rubbing it.

She slipped her hands out from underneath mine and Tyler's and held her glass up. "To Freya and Carter." She smiled.

We all held our glasses up and clinked. We took a sip and sat in awkward silence for a few minutes when the waiter came over.

"Was everything okay for you all?" he asked as he started clearing the plates.

"Was lovely. Thank you," Tyler replied. "Can we have the bill once you're ready, please?"

"Certainly." The waiter smiled and walked away.

"It was lovely seeing you both. You will have to come over to the apartment. We're going to start house hunting soon. We want to move out of the city," I said, making small talk.

"That would be lovely," Laura replied. "Sorry. Please don't think I'm unhappy for you both. It's just a shock. We went through so much to fall, and you know, it's always hard when people fall so quickly and naturally." She swallowed the lump in her throat. "I am happy, really," she said as tears began to fall. "Bloody hormones." She sobbed into her tissue.

I slid out of the booth and wrapped my arms around her, kissing the top of her head. "I know, sweetie. I can't imagine what that must be like." I didn't know what else to say in response. The waiter brought the bill out. Before Tyler could see how much it was, Carter had handed his card over to the waiter, holding his hand up in a no gesture. The waiter was back quickly, handing Carter his card. I heard Tyler thank him and apologise about Laura. I heard Carter talking quietly but I couldn't hear what he was saying as we started to walk out of the restaurant. I looked over my shoulder and watched Carter and Tyler laughing at each other as they started to walk behind us.

We got outside in the cold. "Are you okay?" I asked Laura.

"I'm fine. I'm sorry for my outburst. I really am so

happy for you and Carter." She smiled weakly.

"I know you are." I hugged her and gave her a kiss on the cheek. Carter and Tyler gave their tickets to the valet and waited for our cars to come around. We only had to wait a few minutes and they were parked outside. We said goodbye to Laura and Tyler and got into our car.

"Well, that was eventful," Carter said, raising his eyebrows.

"I know. I feel awful," I said, strapping myself in.

"Why?"

"I didn't know they had such a hard time conceiving. She never said anything."

"Maybe she didn't want to. Maybe she felt she could deal with it on her own."

"Maybe. I just feel guilty." I shrugged

"Don't feel guilty. We are as blessed to have this baby as they are." He started the engine and pulled away.

"I know we are, but you know what I'm like." I smiled.

"You are too caring."

"Thank you for lunch."

"You don't have to thank me. It's your money too."

"It isn't really. We aren't married." I laughed.

"But we will be." He winked. "You'll be mine, legally."

"I can't wait." I beamed.

"Oh, I've had an email from Dr Cox. We're booked in tomorrow, just to have a scan and some blood tests, then they will book our twelve-week scan in." My heart ached seeing how happy he was. I still couldn't believe we were having a baby.

We pulled up at home just after six. I couldn't believe how quickly the day had gone. We were greeted by Julia and James, who were sitting in the lounge, having a cup of tea. They both stood up, placing there cups on the coffee table. Carter shook his head at them and smiled. They both nodded and continued their conversation. I liked them.

We walked upstairs to our room. I dumped my bag down on the chair in the corner and flopped down on the bed. Oh, it felt good. Carter lay next to me. "Are you okay?" he asked.

"I'm tired," I said, yawning.

"How about a nice film tonight?" he suggested.

"Oh, I would like that. My choice though." I beamed at him.

He pushed himself up and lay on his side, resting his head on his bent arm. "Of course." He leaned down and kissed my nose. "Do you want me to get Julia to cook you anything? You've hardly eaten today, and everything you have eaten, you've thrown back up again."

"I'm okay at the moment. I need to get out of these clothes though." I groaned as I got up. Carter moved, sitting on the edge of his bed, undoing his boots. I walked over and shut the door. I kicked my ankle boots off and stood in between Carter's legs, smiling down at him. I lifted my dress over my head. I was wearing a black silk plunge bra. Not that

I needed it, but it made me boobs look amazing. I slipped my tights off and threw them over with my boots. Luckily, I had put my matching silky knickers on.

"Oh, Freya. You are such a dream." He ran his hands down the side of my body then pulled me on top of him, both of us falling back onto the bed. I leaned in to kiss him. He set my soul on fire. As soon as we touched, I needed him. I started pulling at his Harrington jacket. He pushed me away while he took his jacket and jumper off then pulled me back in to him. I teased him with my tongue then kissed him hard. I put my hands in his hair and tugged gently. I wanted him. He rolled me over delicately so he was on top of me, hovering. He kneeled up and undid his belt and jeans and pulled them down. I loved watching him undress. He lowered himself back over me, finding my mouth once more. His hand once again ran down the side of my body. He found my knickers and moved them aside. He smiled when he felt how ready I was for him. He slowly entered me. I moaned out. I didn't know what had come over me, but I felt like I was ready to explode already. He thrust into me slowly; each movement pushed me closer and closer.

"Carter," I moaned as he continued. "I'm going to come," I whispered as he hit my sweet spot again and again. I moaned as my orgasm shattered through my body, Carter following behind, kissing me hungrily as he did. He rolled off me and turned the TV on. What a perfect start to our evening. He grinned.

I climbed out of bed and went into the bathroom. I needed a shower. I was hot and sweaty after our quick fondle. I turned the shower on and watched as the water fell down like a waterfall. I stepped under the burning hot water and let it scald my skin. It was nice being in there on my own, just gathering my thoughts. It had been such a whirlwind of a day. I still couldn't believe we were having a baby. I looked towards the bedroom and smiled. Carter was going to make such a wonderful daddy.

I stepped out of the shower and wrapped myself in a towel. I walked through to our dressing room and picked out my old *Friends* t-shirt and some loose trousers. I didn't like anything feeling tight around my belly. I put my hair into a messy bun and switched the lights off as I made my way back through to our bedroom. Carter was watching *Kitchen Nightmares*.

"Ahem, it's film time," I said cheekily.

"I know. What'll it be?"

"*Twilight*." I beamed at him, jumping in bed next to him.

"Oh, God, no." He shook his head.

"My choice. Yours tomorrow. Chop chop. Put it on," I ordered.

He sighed, got up, and went to the DVD cabinet in the living room. I laughed at the look James and Julia would be giving him. He appeared with the DVD and put it on, giving me the side eye the whole time.

"Are you excited?" I teased.

"Oh, yes. Very much so," he said sarcastically.

"Good!"

I lifted his right arm up and snuggled under it. He held me tight and kissed me on the head.

Perfect. I was excited for tomorrow.

CHAPTER TWENTY-ONE

I sat down at my desk and started working on our new signing. The office was quiet. Most of the office was on their Christmas annual leave. I still couldn't believe how quickly the last two months had gone. I was leaving early that day as we had our twelve-week scan. I was so excited to see the baby again. Last time we saw it, we were only four weeks gone. I had worked it out right. I fell pregnant the day we came home from Paris. We had my parents and Carter's parents arriving that evening as they were spending Christmas with us; it would be our last Christmas in the penthouse, and our last as just the two of us. I smiled at the thought.

Finally, two p.m. came around. The morning had dragged. I logged off my computer. I couldn't wait. Two weeks off with Carter and our families. I loved Christmas.

I stuck my head around the door of Morgan's office.

"Hey, I'm off now. I've sent Carla everything she needs for our new author. Have a wonderful Christmas with

Courtney and your family." I smiled at him. "See you in the New Year."

"Thanks, Freya. Good luck today. Let us know your due date. See you over Christmas." He smiled back at me. I turned and walked out of his office and headed for the lift. As I came to the ground floor, I saw Carter standing in the lobby, smiling at me.

"Ready?" he asked.

"I'm so excited." I kissed him on the cheek.

"Me too, baby. Me too."

The drive to the hospital wasn't too bad. My appointment was at three-thirty. We walked through to the ultrasound department. I told Carter to sit down while I checked myself in.

"Lovely. Miss Greene, take a seat. Dr Cox will call you through shortly."

I smiled at the young receptionist sitting on the front desk. The hospital was beautiful; very modern. Carter had private health and medical insurance so he insisted I go through his hospital.

I sat down and held his hand. "I'm starting to get nervous now."

"It'll be fine. I wonder if baby will be born end of June or end of July."

"I still think end of June. We will see."

"Miss Greene, Mr Cole. Please come through," Dr Cox called.

"Here we go," Carter whispered.

"How are you feeling?" Dr Cox asked me.

"Okay. A bit crampy but I've heard that's normal." I smiled nervously.

"It certainly is." He jotted down some notes. "Any bleeding?"

"No. None." I fiddled with my fingers.

"Perfect. Okay. If you would like to lie on the bed for me. Please pull your top up and undo you trousers buttons." He showed me to the bed and pulled the curtain round. "Once you're ready, call me." I nodded. Carter followed me. I undid my trousers buttons and let out a sigh of relief; I felt like I could breathe.

Carter steadied me as I lay down on the bed and rolled my top up.

"I'm ready, Dr Cox," I called out.

"Please, call me David."

"Sorry." I smiled.

"Okay, this gel I put on is a bit cold, as you know. Sorry," he said.

"It's fine. It's not that cold."

Oh my God. I was so anxious

"Okay, let's see your baby!"

He put the ultrasound scanner on my belly and pushed firmly. *I need a wee so bad.* After a few minutes, David took a deep breath. "Freya, would you mind going to empty your bladder for me?"

I threw a look at Carter.

"Is everything okay, David?" he asked, worried.

"I'm just finding it hard to get a clear shot of the baby. I think Freya's bladder is too full. It's completely normal so please try not to worry." He nodded at Carter and me. Carter helped me up off the bed. I did my trousers up and walked into the toilets.

I walked back into the room.

"Okay, let's try again, shall we?" He smiled at me again.

Now I felt uneasy. I knew deep down something was wrong.

I lay back down and let him continue with the scan. It was taking too long. He had spent about ten minutes moving the ultrasound all around my lower belly. We were all in silence. He took the scanner off my belly and put it back in his holder. He twisted his chair around to face me. "Freya, Carter. I'm so sorry."

I looked at David, trying to read his face. Carter squeezed my hand.

"What's wrong?" I asked, that awful lump creeping up my throat.

"I'm so sorry, but I can't find the baby's heartbeat."

"Can you check again?" Carter said, choking back his tears.

"I can, but your baby is only measuring at nine weeks, when you are actually twelve weeks pregnant, which tells me that your baby has stopped growing." He stood up and looked at me. "I will give you some time. I'll be back in a few moments," David said with a grimace.

He walked out, closing the door quietly behind him.

As soon as the door was shut, I broke down. Carter sat on the edge of the hospital bed, taking me in his arms, neither of us knowing what to say to each other. My heart broke. I turned and looked at the image on the screen. It was our baby. Our perfect baby.

A few moments later, Dr Cox walked back in. I hadn't moved. Carter was still cradling me.

"What's the next step?" Carter asked harshly, his eyes red and swollen from his silent sobs.

"Well, we will send you home for a couple of days. Then you have three options. You can let nature take its course, which can take up to eight weeks. You can have tablets that we insert into your cervix, or you can have the surgery as a day patient. Please do not make any decisions now. Go home and try and enjoy Christmas. I will get Sarah to book you an appointment on the 29th December to come in and discuss your choice. Carter, you have my number. If anything changes in the next forty-eight hours then please call me." He put his arm on my shoulder and gave it a delicate squeeze. "I am so sorry again, Freya."

As he started to walk away, I stood up and followed him. "David," I said, sniffing. "Can I ask you a question?"

"Of course," he replied.

"I thought that if you had a miscarriage that you bleed

and have excruciating cramps." I sniffed again, eyes welling up. My voice was breaking. "That's what my midwife told me. She said I would know if I miscarried."

He sighed and faced me. "Freya, you had a missed-miscarriage. Your baby's heart stopped beating but didn't leave your uterus." He looked down at me with sympathy.

"Why wasn't I told this? Why haven't I been told about this type of miscarriage?" I asked angrily.

"I don't know. You should have been. I'm sorry, Freya, but I really have to go," he said awkwardly. He nodded at Carter and left the room.

I fell to the floor and let out my cry; the cry I had been holding in. Carter came running over and sat down beside me, holding me tight. He was kissing my hair. I could hear him sniffing. "Everything will be okay. It will all be okay," he said through tears of his own. "Come on. Please get up." He lifted me and walked me out of the room. I was numb. The thought of still being pregnant with our baby with no heartbeat was too much.

We got to the car and drove home in silence. Carter had his fist up to his mouth, obviously deep in thought. I couldn't stop the tears from flowing while cradling my tummy.

As we arrived home, Mum and Dad were there. So were Elsie and Ava. We walked through to the lounge area where they were waiting for our news. I walked straight past them all and upstairs, not saying a word to any of them. As

I walked up, I heard Carter talking.

"We've lost the baby. There was no heartbeat." I heard the hurt in his voice. I walked into our bedroom and shut the door. I lay on the bed as I started to cry again. How did I even have any more tears left? My eyes were sore and red. I loved this baby so much; knowing that we would never meet them was tearing me apart. I heard the bedroom door open and I looked over to see my mum and dad.

"Oh, Freya, darling." Mum came over and stroked my hair. "We're so sorry." My dad found situations like this awkward. He sat down on the other side of the bed, patting my back.

"Why us, Mum? Why?" I asked, letting out my sobs.

"Just sometimes things aren't meant to be, darling," she said. "Me and your dad lost three babies before you, all at different stages. It does get easier." She stroked my cheek.

"I don't want to forget the baby, Mum." I sniffed.

"Oh, sweetie. You will never forget. I still think of our three. They are always with me. But look at it this way, if me and Daddy had never lost, we would never have had you." She smiled sweetly at me. "I know it's hard to understand now, but it will all make sense."

I saw Carter standing in the doorway; he looked so broken. Dad nodded towards the door which made my mum turn around.

"Ah, okay. We will go and unpack and get settled. We'll leave you to it." She kissed me on the forehead and wiped a stray tear.

"Love you, baby face," my daddy said as he got up and walked out behind my mum. Carter smiled at them as they walked past.

He walked slowly over to me. "Hey, beautiful." He kissed my forehead.

"Hey." I leaned up and kissed him on the lips. "You okay?"

"Not really. I can't stop thinking about it. I can't stop thinking about you."

"I'll be okay. We will get through this." I stood up slowly. "Come on. It is Christmas, after all." He scooped me up and kissed me. I wrapped my arms around his neck, pulling away to look at him. His eyes were burning deep into mine. He sighed before kissing me one last time.

We walked down the stairs, holding hands. Elsie and Ava smiled weakly at us. "Who's hungry?" I asked, trying to be as cheery as I could.

We all sat down in the dining room after eating a Chinese. Carter and I were originally going to cook, but after everything that had happened, our families suggested us taking it easy.

Carter stood up and held his glass of red up in the air and cleared his throat. "Freya and I would like to thank you for coming and spending Christmas with us. Even though we've had this heartbreaking news today, we really wouldn't want to spend our Christmas any other way. So, thank you for spending it with us," he toasted. We all toasted to him.

Once dinner was cleared away, I put my comfortable pyjamas on and got settled on the sofa in the lounge. I was cuddled up with Carter. Mum and Elsie were lost in conversation, and Ava and my dad were talking about Australia. This was the third time they had met; it was so nice that they all got on well.

"I can't wait until we can see the new house again. Fresh start." I smiled at him.

"I know. Me too," Carter said, his hand automatically going to my belly. I didn't say anything. I didn't want to upset him again.

My mum and Elsie came and sat next to us. "How are you feeling, dear? I know that's a silly question," Elsie said, looking at Carter.

"Don't be silly. I'm not bad, thank you. Looking forward to Christmas. We can deal with all of this after."

"We will make it such a wonderful Christmas, all of us here together."

"That we will," my mum said.

Carter hadn't said much. I knew he was trying to be strong for me, but he didn't need to be. He lost something as well. I took his hand and gave it a squeeze. "Why don't you tell our mums about our new house?" I suggested. I wanted to try and take his mind off it.

He looked at me then back at our mums. "Oh, yeah." He coughed. "Of course. We've bought a house in Surrey.

That way, the commute isn't too bad for Freya and me. It's a beautiful detached house on one and a half acres of land." He smiled at me. "It's six bedrooms, has a swimming pool, study, gym, and a guest house which has three bedrooms, a kitchen, and a lounge, so my wonderful housekeepers have their own space. Plus, enough room for all of you. We should be moving in January." He kissed my hand. I loved watching him speak about something he was so passionate about.

"It sounds lovely, sweetie," Elsie said. "What will you do with this place?"

"I'm not sure yet. We might keep it." He shrugged. "Haven't thought that far ahead."

"Well, I think it sounds wonderful. I can't wait to see it," Mum said. I looked behind her and saw Dad and Ava in deep conversation. I smiled.

"Hey, would you mind if I went to bed?" I asked quietly. "I'm exhausted. It's been such a long day and, to be honest, I'm emotionally drained." My eyes still felt sore.

"Of course, darling." Mum stood up and cuddled me then kissed me on the cheek. Elsie was waiting behind her to also cuddle me and wish me goodnight. I waved goodnight to Ava and went and gave my dad the biggest squeeze. He put his arm around my waist and cuddled me back. "Night, baby face." He smiled up at me.

I looked back at Carter; he mouthed that he would be up shortly. I went to the bathroom and splashed my face. I took a deep breath. I walked into our bedroom and cuddled into my duvet and started to cry. I'd put on a brave face for Carter but I couldn't hold it in anymore.

I cradled my tummy. *I miss you so much, little one.*

CHAPTER TWENTY-TWO

I woke up with a jolt, my hand immediately going to my belly. The lump crawled back up my throat. I had such a bad night. Every time I fell asleep, I woke from a nightmare. Carter wouldn't let me go all night. It was four-thirty a.m. I took a sip of water before lying back down. My mind was racing and I couldn't settle.

Carter had rolled over and was in a peaceful slumber. I was agitated and exhausted. I slipped out of bed and stood looking out of the bedroom window, looking over the beautiful city. I caught my breath as I felt Carter wrap his arms around me. I hadn't even heard him get out of bed.

"Come back to bed, baby," he said sleepily.

"I can't settle. I've had the worst night," I mumbled, turning to face him.

"Please, come." He ushered me back over to the bed and lay behind me, kissing my neck. "Love you."

"I love you too."

He stroked my hair, trying to get me to relax. It was

working because I could feel my eyelids getting heavy. A few more strokes and I was gone.

I rolled over and stretched. I panicked when I couldn't feel Carter next to me. I sat up and looked around the room; he wasn't there. I looked at his clock. It was nine a.m. I sprung out of bed and stood at the top of the stairs. There were red roses placed on every step down to the bottom. Carter walked out of the living room and stood at the bottom of the stairs, smiling at me.

"You coming down?" he asked, still beaming. I was nervous. I held onto the hand rail as I slowly walked down the stairs, taking everything in. The roses smelled amazing. The lights were dimmed, but just enough so I could still see everything. I stepped slowly down the stairs, one by one, not taking my eyes off Carter's. I stepped off the bottom step and took his hand that he held out for me.

"What's all this? Where is everyone?" I asked, my voice shaking.

"They're out, picking up some last minute bits for Christmas." He smiled. He took both my hands. "Freya," he choked. "I love you, so much. I honestly have never, ever felt like I do with you."

He smiled. "After everything that has happened, well, I just love you even more." I was lost listening to him, my heart thumping, feeling like I was falling in love with him even deeper.

"This was always my plan, just not with these circumstances." He looked deep into my eyes, and I watched him eagerly. He took my left hand in his as he slowly dropped to one knee.

"Please, would you do me the extraordinary honour of becoming my wife?" he asked, holding the most beautiful pear-shaped diamond ring I had ever seen. His eyes twinkled looking up at me, waiting for my answer. I felt so overwhelmed by everything, tears started pricking my eyes.

"Yes. Of course, yes!" I exclaimed as he slipped the ring gently onto my finger. I couldn't help staring at it. The ring was stunning. It was a four carat diamond and encrusted by small diamonds either side on a thick platinum band. I started crying. He scooped me up and spun me around as he kissed me passionately. I felt the heat between us growing. I wanted him to take me on the floor. I pulled at his hair as I lost myself in the moment. I heard a noise coming from the kitchen, and there I saw my parents, Elsie, and Ava. Ava squealed with excitement as my mum and Elsie were hugging each other, crying. My dad wasn't letting his emotions out but I could see he was happy.

"Oh, and before you ask, I did ask your father's permission." Carter put me down gently and held my hand, walking us over to our family.

"Congratulations, darling." My mum kissed us both on the cheek, my dad shaking Carter's hand. Elsie and Ava hugged us both, and Elsie had tears in her eyes. I was hoping they were happy tears. Julia had cooked a big breakfast for us all; it was lovely having all the family there.

After breakfast, I wandered back up to the bedroom alone. I sat on the side of the bed and stared at my left hand. I couldn't believe we were actually engaged. It had been such a crazy few months. This was the last thing I expected. I flopped down on the bed and sighed. I felt such a mix of emotions. I wanted to be happy and excited, yet I felt sad and empty. I didn't want to have to lose our baby. I didn't want to go back to being not pregnant. I felt a tear run down the side of my face and onto the duvet. I sniffed as I heard the bedroom door open.

"Hey." I heard Carter's voice, low and soft. "Are you okay?"

"Mmm, just thinking." I smiled, my eyes still filled with tears

"About what?"

"Everything. Our baby, our engagement, us." I looked at him and took his hand.

"We will get through this. I've been thinking this little bundle in here," he said, pointing at my belly, "has been sent to us for a reason, and even though we don't know what that reason is, we will. This baby was just too precious for this world at the moment. They will come back to us. I know it." He leaned down and kissed my forehead, lingering for a few seconds. I loved the spark that ran through my blood, the electricity in my body from his touch, his kiss. I was so deeply in love with him and I didn't want to ever live without him again. As he moved away, I leaned up on my elbows and kissed him. I kissed him as if I was going to lose him. I wanted him to know and feel every emotion that was going through me. His hands were on my face. I didn't want to tear myself away. Carter knelt up and hovered over me, and my breathing slowed. We both looked at each other, knowing what we wanted but neither of us acting on it. Carter smiled and went to get up when I grabbed his t-shirt and pulled him onto me, covering his mouth with mine. My kiss was aggressive, my pent up emotions taking over my body. Carter ran his hand up my top and pulled away as he took it over my head. He threw it on the floor and continued to kiss me, this time a lot more softly. I lifted his t-shirt over his head. He cradled me as he kissed my neck, and I moaned quietly. He silenced me by putting his hand over my mouth. "Shh, it's not just us in the house." He smirked at me. We spent the rest of the morning losing ourselves in each other, again and again.

We all sat in the lounge with the fire roaring as the night drew in, everyone having quiet conversations as Carter and I sat watching the fire burning. I was snuggled into him, his fingers tickling up and down my thigh. I couldn't have wished for a better Christmas Eve. I spent all day with the man I loved and the evening with our family. I hadn't told Laura or Courtney that we had lost the baby. I hadn't even told Brooke I was pregnant, so at least that was

226

one less heartache of explaining. I looked at the time; it was seven-twenty p.m. so, I thought I would give Laura a quick call.

"Hey! You okay? Oh my God, how did the scan go? When are you due?" she asked, not even stopping for a breath.

"Hey, not bad. You?" I answered, pacing myself. I was nervous.

"Yeah, okay. Little madam hasn't stopped wiggling all day today. When are you due?" she asked again.

"Erm, Lau..." I said; the lump in my throat hurt. Carter and my mum looked at me with heartbroken expressions on their faces. I tried to smile, but as I did, a tear made its way down my face. I stepped up and walked through to our dining room where everything had been set up for Christmas Day. I sighed.

"Freya, what's wrong?" I could hear she was panicking

"We lost the baby." I sniffed. I really didn't want to break down on the phone. "We went for our scan yesterday, but the baby had no heartbeat." I swallowed, trying to get rid of the lump. My eyes stung. I wiped my nose on my sleeve and closed my eyes.

"I don't know what to say, Freya. I'm so sorry," she whispered. Her voice was shaking.

"It's okay," I whispered back.

"How's Carter doing?"

"He's putting on a brave face for me. I just don't

understand why it's happened. I had no warning, no signs... nothing. I hadn't even heard of a missed miscarriage." I sighed.

"Neither have I," she replied, still with a shaking voice.

"I've got to go back on the twenty-ninth to make our choice on how to move forward," I said,

"but, I just wanted to call and let you know."

"I'm so sorry. Please send Carter our love," she said quietly.

"We have got some good news as well though." I wiped my eyes. "We're engaged." I smiled.

"Oh, Freya! That is amazing. I'm so happy for you." I could hear that she was smiling.

"Thank you, hun. Anyway, I've got to go. I'm wiped. I hope you all have a wonderful Christmas. I will call you on the twenty-ninth."

"Have a lovely Christmas too," she said.

"Bye."

"Bye. Love you," she said.

I put the phone down and walked back into the lounge. Carter was there waiting for me, giving me a cuddle as soon as he saw me.

We woke early on Christmas morning. I was like a kid. We all sat around the fire, exchanging gifts. I was anxious about giving Carter my present. How do you buy for someone who has everything? I was bought back to the

228

room as Carter placed a medium-sized box on my lap, beautifully wrapped with a big bow. I smiled and kissed him on the cheek. I slowly undid the ribbon and tore the corner of the wrapping paper. The green leather box caught my eye; I knew what this was. I slipped the rest of the wrapping paper off and opened the box delicately. Inside was a beautiful silver Rolex with diamonds round the face. I turned it over to see the back had been engraved: 'Our forever starts today – C x'.

I kneeled up and threw my arms around him. "Thank you so much. It's beautiful." I kissed him softly on his lips.

"You are more than welcome." He smiled at me.

"Okay, okay. Your turn!" I said excitedly.

I handed him a slightly bigger box. Unfortunately, my wrapping was nowhere near as good as his. His eyes lit up as he took it from me and delicately started unwrapping. I saw the smile on his face grow when he saw a familiar green leather box. I laughed as he took the box out of the wrapping paper. I had decided to buy Carter a vintage Rolex set on a black leather strap. I too had it engraved with: "Forever mine, forever yours – F x". He pulled me onto his lap and kissed me.

"What a wonderful gift. Thank you." He smiled, squeezing me as he did.

"You're welcome. It's hard to buy for someone who has everything." I smiled back at him.

"Come. Let's have breakfast. I'm hungry."

We all got up and walked into the dining room, ready for our breakfast together. I felt so grateful. I loved my family so much.

The twenty-ninth was soon upon us. Christmas felt like a lifetime ago. We had such a wonderful day filled with laughter, love, and good food. We sat quietly while we drove to the hospital, knowing this was the end of this little adventure for us. We finally arrived and made our way up to Dr Cox's office. I checked us in with the same receptionist who we saw last time.

"Good morning, Miss Greene. Please take a seat," she said politely.

I smiled and took my seat next to Carter's. He took my hand and held it tightly while we waited. A few moments later, Dr Cox came out of his office.

"Freya, Carter, please come in." He smiled as he showed us into his office. I sat down nervously; I really didn't know what to expect. Again, Carter took my hand as soon as he sat down.

"How have you been feeling, Freya?" he asked.

"No different. Still a bit sick here and there but nothing to be alarmed about, I don't think." I smiled weakly at him. I could hear my heartbeat thumping in my ears.

"Okay, that's good. What have you decided?"

"Well, neither of them sound appealing, but I think it will be the surgery. If that's okay." I squeezed Carter's hand while turning to look at him. He hadn't said anything.

"Of course. If that's what you want. We will do some observations then take you down to have the process started," he said with a grimace. "I will be back in a moment." He got up and left the room, closing the door quietly behind him.

"Are you okay?" I asked Carter.

"Yeah, sorry. Just don't want you having to go through this." His face slackened; his brow furrowed - eyes darting about in concern as if he were searching for a place to hide.

"I'll be fine. We will be able to start again. We both know we want a baby now so what's stopping us from trying again?" I smiled.

"Why are you so wonderful?"

"You make me wonderful."

"You're so brave, my love," he said, kissing my hand.

"I don't feel it. I'm so scared. I don't want to lose this baby. I love it so much already. But, it is what it is. We had no control over this outcome," I said, wiping a tear away.

He ran his hand across my cheek. "I love you so much, Freya."

"I love you too."

We were interrupted as Dr Cox walked in. "Okay, we're ready for you, Freya. Carter, if you could sit in the waiting room, we shouldn't be long."

Carter nodded at him. He scooped me up in his arms and kissed me passionately "I'll be waiting for you." He smiled and kissed me on the lips once more.

"See you soon," I mumbled.

I watched Carter walk out the door, turning round for one last look. I walked slowly over to Dr Cox. "Okay, I'm ready," I said bravely. My insides were sobbing, my heart breaking into a million pieces once more.

As I walked next to him, I placed my hand on my belly and whispered, "Until we meet again, little one."

CHAPTER TWENTY-THREE

It had been a week since everything had happened. The first few days were hard, especially when Dr Cox told us that one of my fallopian tubes had been damaged during the surgery. This meant that conceiving again might be a challenge. I felt as if my world had been turned upside down once more. After a few days, I tried to see the positives and not the negatives. I rolled over in bed and watched Carter sound asleep. I missed my mum and dad; they left on Boxing Day, and Elsie and Ava left the day after. The apartment seemed so quiet with just me and Carter.

I picked my phone up and started flicking through Instagram. I really needed to message Brooke. I had been such a bad friend. Laura saw her quite a bit, but after everything happened with me and Carter, I removed myself from the group. I distanced myself.

I felt Carter stirring next to me. "Morning, beautiful." He smiled and kissed me.

"Morning, you." I smiled back, accepting the kiss.

"How are you feeling this morning?"

"A bit better. Not as sore now. Looking forward to getting back to work."

"You still have another two weeks off. Doctor's orders." He smirked. He held his arm up for me to lay with him. I loved listening to his heartbeat through his chest. I closed my eyes and just listened. We were going to see the house again later. Carter wanted to go and get some measurements and didn't want to inconvenience the designer over Christmas. I pulled myself away and jumped into the shower. My hair was in desperate need of a wash. I ran my hands over my body as I lathered myself, stopping at my tummy. A pang hit my stomach. My emotions were still running high. I still longed to have our baby but we knew it just wasn't meant to be. I let out a sigh as I washed my shampoo out of my hair and ran the conditioner through it. I saw Carter walking into the bathroom, fresh out of bed, his bed hair all over the place. He stepped into the shower with me and kissed my neck while I tried to rinse my hair off. We just stood under the shower, letting the water wash over us, neither of us saying anything. He turned me to face him and kissed me deeply. I draped my arms around his neck and leaned into him.

His arms tightened around my waist. "As much as I would love to stand here all day with you, we do need to be at the house soon." He smiled.

"You came into my shower, Mr Cole, not the other way

round," I teased.

"I couldn't resist. My mind is going crazy with different scenarios I would rather be doing to you now, but, we have to get ready." He smirked.

"Well, I'm done. You still need to actually shower," I said as I stepped out of the shower and over to the sink unit. I started brushing my teeth and was watching him as he washed. Everything about him was dreamy. I wanted to get back in that shower with him and forget about it all, but that'd have to wait until later. I put my toothbrush in my holder and walked into our dressing room. I pulled a pair of my faithful River Island jeans on, and a cotton, black long-sleeved top. I pulled my big knitted jumper out and slipped my Uggs on. I sat down at my dressing table that Carter had bought me. I ran my finger over the edge of the mirrored table and smiled.

I rough dried my hair with the hairdryer then pulled the straighteners out and ran them across the ends. Carter walked through with a towel wrapped around his waist. He made my mouth go dry. He gave me a seductive look while walking past me; he was teasing me.

I put my foundation on, watching him the whole time.

He dropped his towel as he stood in front of his wardrobe. "What to wear, what to wear." He looked over his shoulder and winked at me.

"I would rather you stay like that, if I'm being honest."

I heard him laugh. "Wait 'til later." He smirked again.

He slipped his boxers on and threw on his jeans. He stood for a while, debating on a top, then chose a cream roll neck. He slipped his new Rolex on and smiled as he did the leather band up. I put my earrings in, slipped my engagement ring on, then also slipped my own Rolex on.

"You excited to see our house?" I asked.

"Yeah, I am. I'm looking forward to getting in there now. Only a few more months." He walked over and kissed me on the cheek.

"Me too. I can't wait to start afresh. Maybe once we're in there, we can start trying again," I suggested.

"That sounds perfect. We can have lots of fun trying." He winked at me. My stomach flipped. He held his hand out for me, and I took it and stood in front of him.

"Oh, I do love you, Mr Cole." I beamed. I stood on my tiptoes and kissed him. "Ready?"

"After you, beautiful."

I had my hand in Carter's for the whole journey. He gave my hand a squeeze when we were nearly there. We drove up to the black gates at the front of the driveway. Carter got out and pushed the button on the intercom. He got back into the car and watched the gates open slowly. I took a deep breath as we drove up the long driveway. Within a few moments, we were outside our house. It was a recently re-built modern house. We still wanted to change a few things as they weren't to Carter's taste. He also wanted to tell them to not continue with the nursery that we had planned; it was too raw for both of us.

We walked hand in hand up to the front door. There were three steps that led up to it. As we opened the double oak doors, there was a large hallway with a staircase in the middle which took us to our landing which led to our six rooms. Our kitchen was open plan; we had black granite work tops and high gloss white kitchen cupboards with a family room overlooking the garden. The dining room was off of the kitchen and it had a big bay window. Carter left me while he went around and did his last bits. I wandered into the nursery and flicked the lights on. I stood leaning against the door frame; the decorating had only just begun. The massive windows let the winter sun shine through. It would have been the most beautiful nursery. I wiped my eyes as I stood in silence. I could hear footsteps. I turned around and saw Carter. I smiled weakly, and he wrapped his arms around my waist as he nuzzled into my hair.

He took a deep breath. "This room will be used soon, I promise." He let go of me. "Come on, I'm done. Let's go get some food." He smiled. We walked out of the house, smiling. "What do you fancy?" he asked.

"Pizza!" I answered.

"Sounds perfect."

We had just pulled up outside the restaurant; I was starving. Carter came around to my side of the car and let me out.

"Thank you, but I must admit, James does it so much

better." I laughed.

He threw me a look then chuckled to himself. As we were walking towards the restaurant, Carter's phone rang. He looked at his phone, confused. "Sorry. Let me get this."

"Hello?" he said. "This is him, yes... What?" He ran his hand round the back of the head, pacing up and down. "Right, okay. We will be right there." He grabbed my hand and pulled me towards the car.

"Carter, what's wrong?" I asked, panicked.

"It's Chloé," he said abruptly. Carter started the engine and put his foot down, pulling onto the road.

"Oh my God, Carter. Slow down! What the fuck has happened?"

"Chloé has passed away," he said, looking at me with pain in his eyes.

"She's what?"

"She passed away during child birth," he said anxiously.

"Child birth? Oh my God, Carter! Did you know she was pregnant?" I asked, nerves kicking in.

"Of course I didn't, Freya! This is the first I've heard of it!" he said, raising his voice.

"Don't shout at me!"

"I didn't mean it. I'm just trying to get my head round this all. I didn't know she was pregnant. She must have been pregnant while we were in Paris. She wasn't even showing. I just can't get my head round it." He was rambling to himself.

"Carter, calm down. We will sort this. I promise." I took his hand and ran my thumb across his knuckles. He looked at me, sheer panic and worry in his eyes.

We pulled up outside the hospital. Carter literally abandoned the car over two car parking spaces. I jumped out of the car and followed him. He looked behind me, grabbing my hand and running to the reception desk.

"Where is Chloé Blackwood? I had a call saying she had given birth," he said, his voice shaking. I stood behind him and supported him as much as I could.

"Oh, yes, Mr Cole. Please, level five," the receptionist said, turning back to her computer.

We ran through the corridor; he didn't wait for the lift. He ran up five flights of stairs, and I followed him, trying to catch my breath. I obviously wasn't as fit as him. As we got to the stop of the stairs, I put my hands on my knees, trying to get my breath, my chest was tight. My tummy started aching. I stood slowly and held my hand on my stomach.

"Freya! Oh my God, I'm sorry. Oh, baby," he said, walking over to me. "Are you okay?"

I looked at him. "I just need a minute"

He took my hand and walked towards the receptionist. "Chloé Blackwood," he mumbled. She nodded quietly and showed us to a side room.

"Please take a seat. The doctor will be in shortly." She shut the door quietly and left us in a dull box room.

"I can't believe this," he mumbled, pacing the room.

"Hey, it will be okay. We will face this together." I smiled at him. I walked towards him and held his hands then tiptoed and reached up to kiss him. I wanted him to know I wasn't going to leave him. Even though what we were about to face was so much more than we ever wanted, I knew we would get through this.

"I promise you, Carter. Whatever happens next for us, we will be okay." I placed my hand on the side of his face and stared at him in the eyes.

He sighed. "I know. I love you."

We were interrupted when a young male doctor entered the room. "Mr Cole?" he asked.

"Yes, that's me," Carter replied.

"Can we talk in private?" The doctor eyed me.

"No. This is Freya, my fiancée. What's going on?"

"I'm sorry to say this, but Chloé, unfortunately, didn't make it through childbirth. We had no contact details for parents to call so we ran a DNA test on the baby, which is why we contacted you. You are the baby's father."

I took Carter's hand, holding it as tight as my grip would allow. I felt like the air had been knocked out of my lungs. I looked up at Carter. I couldn't read him; there was no emotion.

"With that being said, the baby is to go to any living family. Do you have a number for her parents?" the doctor asked.

Carter shook his head slowly. "Her dad passed away years ago, and her mum passed last year, just before we met. She is an only child as well."

The doctor looked down at his clipboard. "Okay. So, given the fact that she has no parents, the parental right belongs to you."

Carter slowly bowed his head. "I didn't even know she was pregnant," he mumbled.

"By the sounds of it, neither did she. She came in with bad cramps. We thought it was her appendix at first." He shuffled on his feet. "I know it is a lot to take in. Please take a moment. When you're ready, please come and find me." He threw us a weak smile and walked out of the waiting room.

Carter took a step back and fell onto the sofa that was behind him. He threw his head back and put his hands over his face. I stood watching the man I loved falling apart. The man I loved was now a father to a baby he didn't know existed. We were meant to have this moment. I was meant to make him a father, and him make me a mother, but there we were, waiting to meet our future. I walked slowly towards him and stood between his legs. I looked down at him, his head slowly moving forward. He looked up at me. He put his arms around my waist and held me tight as he rested his head on my chest. I wrapped my arms around his neck and took a deep breath. We stood like that for what felt like hours; he didn't say a word. I moved slightly, and as I did, he slowly stood up, taking my face in his hands. "Please don't leave me. I know this wasn't our plan, but this has happened for a reason. I wanted our baby so much. Nothing will ever replace my love for that little one, and I will never stop loving you. I'm scared. I don't think I have ever been so scared, but as long as I have you beside me, I know we will get through this. It's me and you to the end, baby." He kissed me hard; I could feel his emotions.

As he pulled away, I watched his beautiful sage eyes and smiled. "I will never leave you. We did it once before and I will never leave you again. No, this wasn't our plan, but this is our new adventure and I'm so glad I get to do this with you. I'm terrified, but I'm not leaving. There's a baby that needs us. I love you so much, Carter." I gave him one last kiss before taking his hand and we made our way out of the waiting room. As we walked towards the reception, we saw the young male doctor again, this time holding a precious baby in his arms. He walked over to us, smiling. This was the most bittersweet moment for both of us. We were both terrified. Carter squeezed my hand so tight as the doctor showed us the baby. Our baby.

It's true what they say, I thought to myself. A precious loss, for a priceless gain.

This baby was our gain.

ACKNOWLEDGEMENTS

Thank you to my husband and supportive friends for telling me not to give up. What a rollercoaster it has been.

Leanne, once again, you have been amazing. Thank you for making my book look the way it is. You are wonderful and I am so grateful for your continued support.

Karen, thank you for taking the time for editing my book so quickly and efficiently. I am so glad you were recommended to me.

Thank you for reading the second instalment of my book, Freya and Carter will return in book three.

Please don't forget to review on Amazon.

You can find me on social media:

Facebook: @ashleeroseauthor
Instagram: @ashleeroseauthor

Printed in Great Britain
by Amazon

84014140R00140